"Nothing scares me," Caly said, taking a step back.

Folding his arms across his chest, Jeff rocked back on his heels and studied her. "Not even a kiss?"

"Now see here, you—"

"Ah, Caly, Caly. You jump out of planes without turning a hair, but let a man try to kiss you and you break out in a sweat."

"I am not afraid." She glared at him, wishing that he wasn't so handsome in the moonlight.

"Prove it. Prove you aren't afraid to be alone with me." He didn't move. He didn't have to. His husky voice reached out, caressing her. Drawing her.

"How?"

"Let me touch you . . . kiss you," he said, taking her hands in his. "I won't hurt you, I promise."

She believed him. And when she opened her lips to tell him, he claimed them with his in a kiss that was pure magic. Magic that touched her heart, that whirled her world, that took her breath away. . . .

WHAT ARE *LOVESWEPT* ROMANCES?

They are stories of true romance and touching emotion. We believe those two very important ingredients are constants in our highly sensual and very believable stories in the *LOVESWEPT* line. Our goal is to give you, the reader, stories of consistently high quality that may sometimes make you laugh, sometimes make you cry, but are always fresh and creative and contain many delightful surprises within their pages.

Most romance fans read an enormous number of books. Those they truly love, they keep. Others may be traded with friends and soon forgotten. We hope that each *LOVESWEPT* romance will be a treasure—a "keeper." We will always try to publish

LOVE STORIES YOU'LL NEVER FORGET
BY AUTHORS YOU'LL ALWAYS REMEMBER

The Editors

LOVESWEPT® • 309
Lynne Marie Bryant
Calypso's Cowboy

 BANTAM BOOKS
TORONTO • NEW YORK • LONDON • SYDNEY • AUCKLAND

CALYPSO'S COWBOY
A Bantam Book / February 1989

If you would be interested in receiving protective vinyl
covers for your Loveswept books, please write to this address
for information:

Loveswept
Bantam Books
P.O. Box 985
Hicksville, NY 11802

ISBN 0-553-21984-7

Published simultaneously in the United States and Canada

PRINTED IN THE UNITED STATES OF AMERICA

O   0 9 8 7 6 5 4 3 2 1

One

"I'll kill you, Parks," Caly Robbins shouted up at the twin-engine Beech 99 banking away from her billowing red-and-white parachute.

Damn it all to hell, she cursed under her breath, she should have known better than to trust Brad Parks, that lying sidewinder. But she'd been sprawled in the windowless tail of the plane when he had bellowed that he'd seen smoke and ordered her to jump. She'd bailed out immediately, of course: She was a Smokejumper, and it was her job to get to a fire as soon as possible to stop it from spreading.

She snorted angrily. She wouldn't be fighting a fire this trip, because there was no fire. There *was* a plume of smoke rising from the forest of the Paysaten wilderness below—but it came from the chimney of a cabin nestled in the tall pine trees.

"You're dead meat, Parks," she yelled into the now-empty sky.

Gliding into a turn, she looked down at the safe mountain meadow that Parks had spotted for the drop. Safe, ha! The meadow was dotted with cattle. In four years of jumping she'd landed in trees, snags, water, and muskeg—but never in the midst of a herd of cattle.

Directly under her a massive bull tossed his wickedly horned head. Just her luck. She couldn't even manage to land near an ordinary old cow!

At the last moment she slipped the parachute, brushed over the bull's back, and landed in a tuck and roll that brought her quickly to her feet. The startled bull began to twist in fury as yards of silk engulfed him. Caly yanked the quick release cord on the chute, turned tail, and ran. Equipment banged her legs, hampering her race toward the safety of the trees.

The ton of rage thundered close behind her.

She'd never make it.

She heard more hooves pounding behind her; then a loud crack sounded in her ear. Before she knew what was happening, a horse galloped by and a strong arm caught her around the waist, sweeping her off her feet. Grabbing the rider for support, Caly swung up into the saddle.

Behind her wire-mesh mask Caly's eyes widened in surprise as she stared at the black-haired cowboy of her dreams. Her rescuer looked exactly like the hero of her favorite book, *The Virginian*.

Seconds later her hero dumped her behind a massive pine tree and spun his horse around to face the bull. With a quick snap of the whip, the man flipped the parachute off the animal's horns. The bull shook his head, then charged. At the last minute, the cowboy cracked the whip under the bull's nose. With one final blustery bellow, the bull lumbered back toward the lake. Coiling his whip, the man watched it go; then he kneed the horse over to her.

Her legs trembling in delayed reaction, Caly leaned against a Ponderosa pine for support. The Virginian reined up beside her and swung out of the saddle. Feeling light-headed she decided that with his muscular legs and powerful shoulders he could've dogged that bull flat if he'd wanted to.

He planted himself in front of her, feet apart, looking very much as if he wanted to bulldog her. "Of all the stupid, asinine stunts." He didn't raise his voice, but his mouth was tight with anger. "What in tarnation are you trying to do, kill yourself?"

He towered a good six inches above her. She wasn't used to having to look up at people, given her five-feet ten-inch height. It was a new experience, one she didn't particularly like. Spurred to action by his attack, she straightened. Shucking her Nomex gloves, she whipped off her crash helmet.

"Keep your britches zipped—" She stopped abruptly as she realized what she'd said.

"Well, I'll be doggoned if it isn't a woman," Jeff Adams exclaimed. "A little redhead with freckles, to boot."

His eyes left her speechless. Until now she'd thought that nothing could equal the blue-green color of Emerald Lake. How wrong she'd been!

"I bet they call you Red," he continued, his lips curving into a sensual smile.

The smile jarred her back to reality. "They call me Caly Robbins," she said, gripping her helmet to hide the tremor that swept through her. This man was sexy—and dangerous.

"Pleased to meet you, Little Red Robin."

The hint of laughter in his voice almost made her short hair curl more tightly.

"The last man who called me that wound up with a broken nose," she said in warning, her voice going up a notch. Slowly, deliberately, she lowered the helmet to the ground and clenched her right hand into a fist. "I see yours is in need of rearranging."

"Hey, now. I'm a lover, not a fighter," Jeff said, stepping back and raising his arms chest high. He wanted to laugh at this little wildcat and make her bristle some more, but suddenly he didn't feel like laughing. Instead he wanted to know about the last guy she'd slugged and every other man who'd passed through her life.

Then he realized what was going on. Of course, he thought. The boys had done it to him again. They'd sent him another birthday present.

Raking a hand through his hair, he turned away. He should have been prepared for another surprise. The morning he'd turned thirty he'd awakened to find a woman in his bed, and the boys had been sending him a "birthday woman" ever since. It had become a game. He tried to avoid the boys, and they tried to think up new ways to embarrass him. He thought he'd foiled them by staying out on the range, surrounded by cattle. But he should've known that he wouldn't get away so easily. They'd really done it to him this time. What in hell was he going to do with a woman in the middle of the wilderness?

Swinging around, he was branded by the molten gold of her eyes. What was she thinking, expecting? Hadn't the men told her that nothing ever happened between him and their birthday women? Maybe not. Well, he'd just play along and see what kind of act she'd give. He wondered where the boys had found her. She sure was cuter than any of the other girls they'd fixed him up with. And from the way she was acting, he'd bet his prize bull she'd be a real tiger in bed. "You *sound* dangerous," he said suggestively.

Caly didn't trust the glint in his eyes or the wicked way he smiled. Wetting her lips nervously, she backed away. "I am dangerous." What was the matter with her voice? she wondered.

"And you *look* dangerous too," he said in a lazy drawl. "So I guess I'll just have to call you Li'l Red."

"Now, you look here—"

"I am looking." His smile widened. "And you definitely do have red hair. Not that red really does it justice. It's the color of that Ponderosa next to you, the one that's been stripped."

His voice caressed her and his eyes deepened in color, making her wonder if he intentionally had used the word *stripped*. Caly ran a nervous hand through her hair, fluffing it up where it had been flattened by her helmet. Then, realizing what she was doing, she dropped her hand and stared at the ground.

"I'm not little," she muttered.

"You are to me."

He was right. He was one of the few men she'd met who was tall enough to call her little, and that sure didn't make it any easier for her to accept.

"But don't worry," he continued in his sexy drawl. "I like my women short and cuddly. Are you cuddly, Li'l Red?"

Before she realized he'd moved, he was standing up against her, hands behind his chaps, pelvis tilted forward. He was solid, muscular, and all male. Caly fell back a step.

He swaggered forward again, a wicked smile on his face. "Shall we find out?" He raised his hands to hold her head still as he lowered his mouth.

Surprise kept Caly motionless as his lips covered hers. This couldn't be happening, she thought. Her Virginian couldn't be kissing her. Not so soon. But he was . . . and with lips that were firm and mobile and persuasive. Chills of anticipation ran through her—the same chills she got while waiting for her first parachute jump at the beginning of the season. Only these chills were better, much better.

Her knees quivered, and she swayed toward him. Without conscious thought her hands slid around his shoulders, pulling him closer. Her lips softened, moving in response as he nibbled and savored them. He tasted of salt. And man.

She murmured her appreciation, caught up in the new sensations.

Then his tongue probed, demanding entrance. She

gasped, startled by his action. Brad Parks had kissed her the same way, and she hadn't liked it one bit.

Breaking from him, she caught a glimpse of his satisfied smile. Then, swinging her arm as hard as she could, she landed a haymaker under his left eye. He staggered backward but didn't fall on his butt, as Brad had when she'd punched him in just the same way.

Caly stood her ground, shaking her smarting fist as she watched him anxiously. This man wasn't one bit like Brad, she realized. He was a mountain cat, and she had dared to provoke him.

The Virginian swore succinctly, fingering his eye. "Why, you little wildcat! What's the matter? Were you expecting champagne and roses?" He shoved his hands into the back of his chaps, holding himself in rigid check. "Well, tough luck, ma'am. The only thing you'll get is me. The boys must have paid you big bucks to jump in here and help me celebrate my birthday." His smile did nothing to reassure her. Neither did his eyes. His right eye had turned glacial green and his left was rapidly swelling shut. "So come on now, fork out. I'd like to be able to tell them you were worth it."

He swaggered forward. Caly retreated.

"You're making a mistake," Caly said, feeling as if she'd come in on the tail end of a joke told at her expense.

"There sure has been a mistake. I should've known that redheads have sharp claws." He touched his left cheekbone with his middle finger. "Or in your case, a wicked right hook. But believe me, I won't make that mistake again." He bore down on her, his muscles rippling with the smooth grace of a cougar.

She took another step away from him, stammering, "But you don't understand. I'm a Smokejumper. We were flying back to base and mistook the smoke from your cabin for a fire, so I jumped."

Jeff stopped short. "A Smokejumper?" He studied

her carefully, taking in her gear. She was a Smoke-jumper, all right. How in hell could he have missed it?

"You're not a—" He broke off abruptly. Something told him she wouldn't appreciate knowing what he had thought she was. And if he tried to explain, it would only make matters worse. "You're just a Smokejumper?"

"Yes," Caly assured him fervently. She really didn't want to tangle with him. Big Red had taught her to take care of herself around men, but she would come out second best with this cowboy. No doubt about it. Nervously she unstrapped the reserve parachute and her orange ditty bag and dropped them on the ground.

"But you're a woman!"

"So?"

"Women aren't Smokejumpers."

"You're way behind the times, cowboy." She glared at him. Her father had been a Smokejumper, and she had joined up as soon as she could. It made her feel closer to the man she barely remembered. She hoped that somehow he knew what she had chosen to do and was proud of her. "I've been with the outfit four years."

"Of all the stupid, asinine things I've ever heard of!" The cowboy raked an impatient hand through his black curls. "Women have no business being Smokejumpers."

Caly squared off, hands on hips. "Are you saying that I shouldn't be a Smokejumper because I'm a woman?"

"Damn right! Fighting a raging fire is no work for a woman. That's a man's job."

"And a woman's job is looking after a husband and children." Her voice was sharp with sarcasm.

He shook his head. "I didn't say that."

"Well, you meant it. I know your kind."

"But—"

"Let me tell you something, cowboy, so you'll get it straight." She tapped her boot for emphasis. "I'm a fire fighter, and I'll be a fire fighter until the day I die."

Something touched her shoulder, distracting her.

Turning, she found the horse standing behind her. She knew that the animal had sensed her distress and had come to give her support. Patting his neck gratefully, she kept a wary eye on the cowboy. She realized that she probably was overreacting, but she'd finally met a man who was making her wonder about the promise she'd made when she was seven. Maybe there was more to life—no, she wouldn't think about it.

"So you're a rough, tough fire fighter, huh?" the cowboy asked, moving forward.

"Damn right," she said, very aware of his nearness again. She wanted to run, but stood her ground, tangling her fingers tightly in the horse's mane.

"Dead wrong." He brushed two fingers across his lips, hiding a grin. "Underneath that tough tomboy act, you're a soft, sensitive woman."

She gasped at him in surprise. "You're crazy. Soft? I'm not soft."

"We'll see, Li'l Red, we'll see."

The Virginian studied her carefully, thoroughly, touching every part of her with his eyes, as if he were seeking the softness. She moistened her lips nervously. He nodded slightly and let his lips turn up into a full smile. For a moment her guard slipped and she felt a warmth growing inside. Fighting the feeling, she turned to pet the horse again.

"Yeah, well, if a miracle should ever happen and I turn into a soft, clinging woman, you won't be around to see it," she muttered into the horse's mane.

"Hmmmm. So, where 'bouts are you stationed?" he asked.

"At the North Cascades base."

"Say, how about that! I live near Winthrop."

Caly closed her eyes, wondering about fate. Opening them, she turned to find the cowboy smiling broadly with an I-told-you-so expression on his face.

"Why haven't I seen you around town?" he continued. "It isn't all that big."

Caly dug her fingers into the horse's mane. "I've been too busy on the fire lines to spend time in town," she said. "Besides, Winthrop is so full of tourists, you wouldn't have noticed me even if you'd seen me on the street."

"I'd have noticed you, all right, ma'am. You'd better believe it." He touched his eye gingerly. "So, you've jumped in here to fight a fire that doesn't exist. You've successfully defended your honor against a poor, misguided cowboy. Now what are ya gonna do?"

His question spurred her to action. Reaching into the side pouch on the leg of her jump suit, she pulled out a radio.

"I'd better report in to base," she said as she tuned the dials to the correct frequency. Normally the plane would still be circling overhead, but they'd been returning from a big fire near the Canadian border and had only enough fuel for one pass over the drop area. And normally Brad Parks wouldn't have been the spotter, but the regular spotter, Tennessee Sommes, was also a fire boss and hadn't wanted to leave the base totally depleted of manpower, so he'd ordered Brad and Caly, the last two on the jump list, home. Brad had immediately assumed command, and the rest was history.

She should've known that Brad was itching to get even for what had happened during training camp in Missoula. Now, though, none of her anger at Brad was reflected in her tone or her words as she spoke to Zeke Olsen, the base manager. She'd handle her own battles in her own time.

Jeff watched her closely, and when she finished her terse report, he held out his lean brown hand for the radio. Startled, she passed it over without comment.

"Zeke, Jeff Adams here. I'll bring your Smokejumper out with me in a couple of days."

So his name was Jeff Adams, she thought, then sputtered her objections. The radio crackled and Zeke replied. "Sure glad you're up there, Jeff. Take care of her. She can do with a couple days' rest. She's one of our best smoke-eaters, and she's worked a whole lot of fires lately. I'd hate for anything to happen to her. Over and out."

Snapping off the radio, Jeff returned it to her, watching her warily with his good eye. The other was now swollen completely shut.

"Why are you spitting fire at me?"

"You really are a . . . a . . . chauvinist, Mr. High-and-Mighty Jeff Adams."

"What?"

"You had no right to make that decision for me. I'm packing out of here first thing tomorrow morning," she said, golden lights snapping in her amber eyes.

"What?"

"I can't stay here for two days. They need me back at camp. I'd go now, but it's too late." She waved her hand at the dark forest. "But I'm going at dawn, and you can't stop me."

"Now, hold your horses just a doggone minute. They need a fire fighter with two good legs, and you won't fit the bill if you try to walk out of here." He stabbed a long, tanned finger at the mountains to the south. "It's over twenty-five miles to the nearest road. Twenty-five miles of terrain so rugged, a mule thinks twice about crossing it, and normally mules don't have any sense a-tall. You sure'n hell aren't going to walk out of here, and that's that."

"We'll see," Caly muttered under her breath, not trusting herself to speak for fear she'd start screaming at him. Who did he think he was, bossing her around? No one bossed her. She wheeled to head for the meadow. With one lithe movement he cut her off.

"Where d'ya think you're going, ma'am?"

Drawing herself up to her full height, she tried to stare him down, but the arrogant cowboy wouldn't be intimidated. Her right foot itched to plant itself in the middle of his kneecap.

"To rescue my fire pack, if that's all right with you, Mr. High-and-Mighty Jeff Adams," she said sarcastically, waving her hand at the crescent-shaped lake that lay between the meadow and a forested mountain. There was still enough light to see the white chute floating on the pewter-colored water.

"No, it isn't all right with me, ma'am," Jeff said. "You're not walking out there and scaring my cattle off to Canada. They've had enough excitement for one day. I'll collect your gear, but first we have to come to an understanding."

"I understand you, all right. You're a—"

"Ma'am, I'm getting a mite tired of your calling me names. You can call me Jeff, or hey, you, or honey, but I don't answer to 'Mr. High-and-Mighty' or any other such name. Got that?"

His voice had gone very low. She got the message. There was just so much this cowboy would take from her. She nodded sullenly and dropped her gaze, unable to look at the mess she'd made of his eye.

"And I want your promise that you won't try to walk out of here in the middle of the night."

"I could hike out of here easily. I've covered ground a hundred times worse," she said rebelliously.

"Yeah, I know. You're real tough. But I have news for you, Li'l Red. You're exhausted."

"What?" Caly asked, startled, as his large hands closed over her shoulders.

"You're doing a heroic job of hiding it." His smile mocked her. "But the fact is, you're almost out on your feet, and you haven't even been fighting a fire today."

"I just got back from one last night. And before that—" She stopped, feeling foolish that he'd goaded her into defending herself.

"I rest my case." He could feel her tension through the padded suit, and without thinking he began massaging the tight muscles of her shoulders. She put her hands up to stop him, then groaned as his fingers worked their magic.

"When was your last day off?" he asked.

She closed her eyes, wondering for a moment. "The first of June. It's been a real bad year."

"And it's going to get worse if we don't get rain."

She sighed. "Yeah."

"So don't be such a stubborn fool, Li'l Red. Take these couple of days to rest while you've got the chance." His voice was persuasive. "You deserve it. Even Zeke says so."

The exhaustion, which she'd been holding at bay for days, swept over her. She didn't have the energy to lift her head, let alone fight him any longer.

"All right, I'll wait and ride out with you."

"Good. Now that that's settled, the next thing on the agenda is to get your gear off. You're scaring poor Buck here."

Before she realized what was happening, he captured both of her slender wrists in one large hand and began lowering the zipper of her jumpsuit.

"What the bloody hell do you think you're doing?" she yelled, trying desperately to free her hands. Her struggles were totally ineffective.

Jeff saw the fear in her eyes and smiled at her reassuringly. "Easy, now, Li'l Red. I'm not going to hurt you."

Realizing instinctively that he wouldn't hurt her, Caly decided to go along with him. Besides, she'd look like a fool if she kicked up a fuss.

His index finger burned a path between her breasts as he trailed it behind the zipper. She shivered, wondering if she had made the right decision—or if she was playing with fire.

He glanced up and smiled, then lowered his gaze to the zipper. Slowly, slowly it edged downward, finally reaching her tiny waist. He splayed his hand under the suit, over her tummy. She gasped and swayed toward him. He looked at her through thick spiky lashes, then eased his hand out.

He found one leg zipper. Inch by torturous inch he drew it down. His finger caressed the inside of her firm thigh and muscular calf.

"What . . . what . . ." She gasped, wanting to jerk away but wanting to stay too.

"Ssh, easy, now."

He reached for the other leg zipper. She trembled. He touched. She quivered. Heat swept up her legs to pool between them. What was happening to her? she wondered.

Her knees buckled, and Jeff caught her against his long, hard body.

"Not soft, huh?" he murmured into her ear.

Caly knew he was right. She *was* soft, soft and ripe. She was a woman wanting a man for the first time in her life, and all he was trying to do was teach her a lesson.

"Damn you," she said, pushing against his chest.

He let her go. Stepping back, he raised his hands in surrender.

"Okay, Li'l Red. Finish up."

Shaking with anger and with wanting, Caly tore off her jump suit. Flinging it to the ground, she glared at him.

Amusement sparkled in his good eye, and his white teeth flashed. "I can see now that you weren't planning to seduce me, Li'l Red. You definitely aren't dressed for the part."

Hurt replaced anger as she looked down at herself. He was right. The muddy-green Nomex pants had been large for her at the beginning of the season, and she always lost weight on the fire line. Now the baggy pants could hold two of her, and her belt, which she'd cinched tightly around her tiny waist, barely held them up. Her yellow shirt clashed with her hair, but it was fire-resistant, and that was what counted.

She was a fire fighter, not a beauty queen.

She wheeled away, fighting unexpected and unwanted tears. she never cried, and this . . . blasted cowboy wouldn't make her cry—even if he was the Virginian.

Catching a glimpse of her tears, Jeff felt as if he'd been gored. Hell! He hadn't meant to hurt her. He'd do anything to take back his words. She definitely wasn't tough. She was a sensitive woman hiding from the world.

Placing a hand on her shoulder, he swung her around. She stood, head down, shoulders slumped, not bothering to fight. Lord, what had he done?

Two

"Hold your horses, Li'l Red, I didn't mean to hurt you. I was laughing at myself, not you," Jeff said gently.

His thumb moved slowly along her firm jaw to her small, shell-like ear, then feathered across her cheek. She raised startled eyes.

"Lord, you're beautiful," he whispered huskily as he traced her trembling lips.

She jerked back, slapping his hand away.

"Who do you think you're kidding?"

"But—"

"Touch me again, cowboy, and you'll lose your roping hand." Her amber eyes sizzled with fury.

Jeff raked his hand through his hair, then dropped it to his side. Man, was he in deep trouble. Trying to stay on top of his emotions around the little wildcat was worse than topping a bronc.

Fighting for control, he drew a deep, ragged breath. "Yes, ma'am. Anything you say, ma'am." Turning to the waiting horse, he swung into the saddle. "I'll go round up your equipment, ma'am, and give you a chance to cool off."

Watching him ride away, Caly wondered if her world

would ever be normal again. How could he turn it upside down with just the touch of his hand and a smile? She couldn't let him guess how he affected her. It would be too dangerous.

She had never felt the way Jeff Adams made her feel. But then, she had never let a man get as close, either, she realized. The only man who'd tried to cross the line was Brad, and he was about as seductive as a toad.

Jeff was dangerous because everything about him appealed to her—his black hair, his smiling eyes, his long legs, and . . and to make matters worse, he was only teasing, trying to prove that she was soft.

She couldn't let him succeed. She had to remain the tough tomboy. Be one of the boys, she told herself; treat him like one of the boys. It was the only way she'd survive two days. Alone. With her Virginian.

But what would happen if she let down her guard and— No. She wouldn't think about it.

Prodding herself into action, she gathered up her parachutes, jump suit, and ditty bag and carried them through the trees to the small log cabin.

Jeff arrived moments later, dragging the box containing the fire pack at the end of a rope.

"Thank you," Caly said, smiling up at him gratefully. He really was a knight of the range, first rescuing her and now her equipment.

Her smile widened as she watched her gallant Virginian watching her. He sat there with a stunned look on his face. For a moment she wondered what he was thinking. Then, deciding it was probably best that she didn't know, she shrugged and knelt to open the box.

Jeff sat on his horse in a state of shock. This couldn't be happening to him, he told himself; it just couldn't be. Not so fast. And especially not with a gal like Caly. He needed a woman he could cherish and protect, and there was no doubt in his mind that Caly would object to the protection bit. But ready or not, it was happening, and there was nothing he could do about it. She'd smiled and he was a goner.

He *couldn't* let it happen. Not yet. He needed more time. He should turn tail and run. Instead, drawn by a force he couldn't control, he swung down beside her, watching her as she dug through the soggy box.

As Caly shook out her sleeping bag and stretched it on the ground, she wondered uneasily where she was going to spend the night. Definitely nowhere near a certain sexy cowboy, she knew. He was standing over her, making her feel clumsy as she hauled out the shovel, the crosscut saw, and the Pulaski, a digging tool that was a combination of hoe and ax. Jeff took the tools from her and stacked them against the corral, then returned to watch her again. His presence unnerved her, and by the time she reached the canned food, she was fumbling with things.

Jeff picked up a tin of beans, then hobbled out of the way as a can of peaches bounced off his big toe. "Hey, you still mad? Can we call a truce? At least till after we eat."

Sitting back on her heels, Caly studied him. "Okay. Truce," she said, wishing she could read him better. Taking a deep breath, she blurted out in a rush, "I'm sorry I slugged you. I could've found another way to make you stop kissing me."

He touched his swollen eye gently. "Like stomping those lethal boots on my toes or kicking me in the shins?"

"How did you—" She stopped, biting her tongue.

He shook his head sorrowfully. "You know, I didn't think the kiss was all that bad. It appears as if I've been stuck up here so long, I've lost my touch." He stepped forward. "Maybe I need some more practice."

Caly scrambled to her feet, ready to flee, but was stopped by his soft chuckle. "Maybe I should wait awhile. I like my women willing, and you're not willing, are you?"

He smiled wickedly, and Caly realized that he'd been teasing.

Fighting to control her temper, she picked up her jump suit and fished inside for the pack-out bag she carried in the seat for extra padding. Hearing his snort of laughter, she stared down at the suit and the bag, utterly mortified.

No wonder he'd laughed at her earlier. She must have looked like a big-bottomed ape.

"Leave that," he ordered, all traces of laughter gone from his voice. "Let's eat. Bring along that can of peaches. We'll have them for dessert."

In no mood to argue, Caly picked up the can of peaches and plodded after Jeff as he led Buck toward the corral. Two other horses greeted Buck with nickers and Caly with eager noses.

Obligingly, she petted them while Jeff unsaddled and brushed down Buck. When he removed his leather chaps and hung them on the fence, she forgot all about the horses. Jeff's soft jeans fit his long legs like a second skin, showing off his muscular thighs and more. Much more.

He definitely was all man.

Glancing up, Caly saw Jeff watching her, and she knew, as sure as the sun set in the west, that he had read her thoughts.

He cocked his head, raised an eyebrow, and grinned at her. Then he turned and sauntered toward the cabin. Caly stumbled after him, her gaze on the ground, her face flaming.

"Wait till I light the lantern," he called from inside the cabin. Moments later white light spilled out the open door. Entering the room, she slowly looked around. The light from a Coleman lantern, hanging from one of the ceiling beams, revealed primitive furnishings. There were a plank table, two log stumps to serve as chairs, a cot, and a box stove that was throwing off so much heat, she wished she could stay outside.

The smell coming from the cast-iron pot that Jeff was stirring changed her mind. Her stomach rumbled its agreement.

Jeff glanced up and grinned. "Good thing the stew didn't burn." Her stomach growled again. "I'd just put it on to heat when I heard your plane."

That explained why he hadn't been wearing his black Stetson when he rode to her rescue. It was lying on the table. She placed the can of peaches next to it.

"Sit down, and I'll dish up our dinner," Jeff continued, waving at one of the stumps.

Dishing up consisted of plunking two tin plates, some flatware, and the stew pot in the middle of the makeshift table. After pouring coffee into tin cups and digging a loaf of bread out of the box on the floor, Jeff sat down on the other stump.

Caly heaped her plate with stew, and, with no thought of waiting for the cowboy, she forked in a mouthful. Her mouth flew open. Fanning it, she swallowed quickly, then cooled things off with a chunk of bread.

"Hot," she choked out when she could finally breathe. "But good." Wiping the tears from her eyes and the sweat from her face with her sleeve, she proceeded with caution. It was delicious, and before she knew it her plate was empty.

"Have some more."

Jeff pushed the stew pot toward her, and she helped herself, checking to make sure she was leaving enough for him.

With her stomach partly satisfied, she ate more slowly, uncomfortably aware that Jeff was trying to keep from laughing at her. His amusement made her nervous, and she remembered again her resolve to treat him like one of the boys.

"I didn't know there were any grazing allotments in the Pasayten wilderness," she finally said, wondering if he was one of those strong, silent cowboys. She was used to silence. Big Red had always said that a body shouldn't talk just because he was in love with the sound of his voice. Usually she didn't talk much either, but she couldn't keep quiet that night.

Jeff finished his last bite of stew before answering. "There are a few left." He drained his coffee and poured them both another cup before continuing. "When the wilderness act was passed in sixty-eight, only the ranches running stock on their allotments were allowed to keep them. The Half Moon Ranch has been using this pasture for over forty years."

Spooning a second helping of stew on his plate, he pushed the pot back to her. "Finish it up."

"Isn't it a hassle bringing the cattle all the way up here?" she asked, scraping the pot clean.

"I guess you could call it a hassle. We have to wait until July before the snow melts and we can trail the herd in." He chewed and swallowed another piece of meat. "And we can't bring them in by truck, because motorized vehicles aren't allowed in the wilderness. But at least the grass is good, and we don't have to worry about water, so I'd say it evens things out."

She glanced up at him, then lowered her eyes quickly, shifting on her stump. "So you've just brought the cattle in?" she asked thoughtfully.

"Yeah. The day before yesterday," he responded, too busy eating to realize he was being set up.

"You poor, hard-done-by cowboy. You gave me the impression that you'd been stuck out here for ages and ages all by your lonesome."

Jeff looked up. Caly smiled smugly. She had the satisfaction of watching a blush rise from the open collar of his shirt.

"I had to finish checking the fences and clear up some deadfall and make sure the cattle were settling down. . . ." He verbally stumbled to a halt, feeling sheepish.

Pleased she had scored a point, Caly lay down her fork. She ran her fingers through her damp hair, wishing again that it wasn't so hot. How could he stand to live here? she wondered, looking around the cabin. Her cabin at Emerald Lake was a palace compared to this. "Do you like being a cowboy?" she asked curiously.

"Sure do. Can't think of anything I like better." He grinned wickedly as he added, "Except maybe one thing."

Deciding she didn't want to touch that one, Caly concentrated on the last of her stew. But she couldn't keep her eyes off him. The lamplight made the wings of hair over his ears shine like the back of a crow. His expressive lips looked strong and tender. She knew just how soft and sexy they could be.

Unconsciously she began whistling under her breath as he looked at her with a strange expression on his face.

Maybe he was still mad. She had hit him and had gotten away with it. Somehow she knew that was a first. She was a woman, however, and a gentleman didn't hit a woman, even if he had just cause. And Jeff was a gentleman, just like the Virginian.

"What are you thinking?" he asked as various expressions flitted across her face.

"That you look like the Virginian."

"Who's he?"

She teetered forward on her stump. "How can you live in Winthrop and not know who the Virginian is?"

"Oh, you mean the book. The one that fellow Wister wrote?"

"Right."

"I'm not a storybook hero, you know. I'm just a man," he muttered, touching his eye before he continued to eat.

Sweat trickled down the back of her neck and between her breasts. "Can't we do something about your eye?" she asked. "Would cold water help?"

He shook his head. "Not much we can do now. It'll go away eventually."

His eyes reminded her of Emerald Lake, and she was so sorry she'd blackened one.

"I'm sorry," she said.

A smile twinkled in his good eye. "It's okay."

She looked away, embarrassed.

"You sure can cook up one mean stew," she blurted out when she couldn't stand the silence any longer.

He glanced up from mopping his plate with his last piece of bread. "It wasn't really very good. You were starved," he said, realizing she'd just complimented him.

"Hmm, the man's modest. It was gourmet. Beats anything I've ever made."

"So you don't cook?"

"No." She was nothing if not honest. "Big Red, my grandfather, was the cook in the family." He had done all the cooking when they were alone, and during fire season she either boarded or ate in restaurants when she wasn't in camp.

"Was?" he asked, rocking back on the stump.

"He died this spring."

"I'm sorry."

"So am I. I miss him terribly." She propped her chin on her clenched fists and stared down at his black Stetson, which was still lying on the table. "He died in our cabin at Emerald Lake, and I think he was happy. He sure didn't want to die in some hospital bed." She looked up, a smile trembling on her lips.

Rocking forward, Jeff reached out to touch her but changed his mind and picked up the can of peaches instead. After opening the lid with a knife, he speared one peach with his fork and motioned for her to do the same.

"You said you've been with the Smokejumpers four years. When did you first start fighting fires?"

"Twelve years ago."

"Twelve years! You're not old enough."

Caly grinned at his incredulous tone "I'm twenty-five. My grandfather was a fire fighter, and he took me to my first fire when I was thirteen," she explained, remembering how proud she'd been when Big Red finally had allowed her to accompany him.

Jeff stared at her, dumbfounded. "Thirteen!" he said.

"You were only a child. What in tarnation was your grandfather thinking? Why, you could have—"

"Now, just you wait a minute." Slamming her fork down, Caly jumped to her feet, eyes blazing, and knocked over the stump she was sitting on. "I won't have you mean-mouthing Big Red."

Jeff rocked back on the stump, holding up his hands. "Hey, there. Take it easy. Don't start a fire with those eyes of yours." Lowering his hands, he spoke gently, as he would to a spooked colt. "I'm sorry, Caly. I didn't mean to be disrespectful of your grandfather. You obviously loved him very much."

"He was the best grandfather in the world." Realizing she had reacted far too emotionally, she righted the overturned stump and sat down.

"But I can't understand why he would let his thirteen-year-old granddaughter fight fires," Jeff said carefully.

"He didn't have a choice. My parents died when I was seven, so he had to look after me." She paused, remembering the day when her parents had been killed by a fire and her whole world had seemed to stop. Shaking away the memories, she continued, "Besides, I was full grown by the time I was twelve, and everyone thought I was a man."

"You mean he passed you off as one of the boys?" Jeff asked, trying hard to keep all expression out of his voice.

"Uh-huh."

"And you got away with it?"

"Uh-huh." Raising her arm, she wiped the sweat off her forehead with her sleeve.

"What a shame," he said, thinking of his mother and three sisters. There was no mistaking the fact that they were women. "I still think it's too dangerous for women to be running around in the forest fighting fires," he added, shaking his head.

Noting the concerned expression on his face, Caly bit back a scathing remark. Heavens, he was worrying about her.

"It isn't dangerous if you know what you're doing," she said, trying to reassure him.

"It's a hell of a lot more dangerous than most ordinary jobs. Why can't you do something safer?"

"Fighting forest fires is the only thing I know how to do. The only thing I want to do," she said quietly.

When she had grown older, Big Red had encouraged her to take up another profession but hadn't pushed the issue when she'd refused. He knew how important it was to her. A forest fire had killed her parents, and she had dedicated her life to fighting fires.

Jeff missed the intensity in her voice. He was too caught up in feelings of his own. "And you're a Smokejumper, to boot. Do you have a death wish, or something?" he asked impatiently.

"Of course not. What makes you say such a thing?"

"Because you're courting death, that's why. People get killed all the time jumping out of planes."

She shook her head. "Only two Smokejumpers have been killed in parachute accidents, and that's a pretty good record, considering we've been in existence for over forty-five years."

Jeff snorted, not impressed. "So what made you decide to become a Smokejumper? Wasn't being a regular smoke-eater dangerous enough?"

She could have told him how proud she was to be one of the elite group of three hundred Smokejumpers, but that would have sounded too corny, as if she were blowing her own horn. So she said instead, "I'm a Smokejumper for the same reason you're a cowboy. I love it. I enjoy the camaraderie, the feeling of doing an important job and doing it well. But more than that, I love the wilderness, walking where no one has ever walked before."

Watching her amber eyes shine with enthusiasm and her face glow with happiness, Jeff bit back further protest. Instead he started on a new tack. "I still can't figure out why you jumped in here. I thought the Forest Service didn't fight fires in the wilderness."

"Normally that's the case, but it's been so hot and dry this year that they've decided to contain them. Especially if they're anywhere near the Canadian border."

"Okay, that explains why you're here, but where's your partner?"

Caly wiggled on the stump again, feeling uncomfortable. "He was sick."

"Great. He let you jump alone. Some partner." He shook his head in disgust. "On second thought, why should I complain because you're here . . . all alone?" He smiled a thoroughly masculine smile that sent shivers down her spine. ". . . With me."

His good eye roamed over her, making her very aware of the way her damp shirt clung to her breasts and of the fact that she never wore a bra. It also made her very aware of the heat that intensified between her legs.

Suddenly Caly realized just how vulnerable she was. She'd been alone with men on many occasions and had never given it a second thought. But she'd never been attracted to any of the men the way she was toward this cowboy—and that could spell trouble. Big trouble. She had to get away from him.

Jumping to her feet, she bumped into the table before rushing to the door.

"It's hot in here. I think I'll step outside for a breath of fresh air." Her excuse sounded phony even to her, as if she were some high-falutin' society girl waving her fan, but she was past caring whether he laughed at her.

It was a little cooler outside, but not much. The night air retained most of the day's heat. A full moon, sitting above the mountain ridge, glowed eerily through the smoky haze that clung to the trees and meadow. She'd seen similar nights before, but this night was almost unreal. It fit right in with everything else that had happened since she'd jumped out of the plane.

Jeff joined her, laughing softly. "What's the matter? Something frighten you?"

"Nothing scares me." She rubbed her damp palms on the sides of her pants.

"Nothing, huh?"

"Nope."

Folding his arms across his chest, he rocked back on his heels, studying her. "Not even a kiss?"

"Now see here, you—"

"Ah, Caly, Caly. What a shame. You jump out of planes without blinking an eye, but let a man try to kiss you and you break out in a sweat."

"I am not afraid." She glared at him, wishing that he didn't look so handsome in the moonlight. If she knew what was good for her, she'd keep on running, right down the mountain and as far away from him as possible.

"Prove it. Prove that you aren't afraid to be alone with me." He didn't move. He didn't have to. His husky voice reached out, caressing her, drawing her.

"How?" she whispered as all thoughts of fleeing vanished.

His large hands caught hers, holding them loosely. "Let me touch you . . . kiss you." His hands slid up over her wrists, his thumbs smoothing her skin. "I won't hurt you. I promise."

She stared up at him, believing him. Despite his suggestive words in the cabin, her Virginian was a gentleman. He wouldn't force himself on her or make her do anything she didn't want to do.

Jeff lowered his head slowly, watching for signs that she was ready to punch him again. When she moistened her lips, he smiled, then brushed them lightly with his.

The kiss was pure magic. Magic that touched her heart, making it pound madly . . . then skip . . . then stop. Magic that spun her world around. Magic that took her breath away. When the world stopped spinning and she started breathing again, she pulled his head down, demanding more.

He gave her more. His tongue teased her lips. She

parted them willingly. He entered slowly, brushing across the roof of her mouth, then filling her completely. Her knees gave out, and she slumped against him.

He held her close, branding her with his heat and strength, branding her with a hardness that pressed against her pelvis, making her conscious for the first time of the power she could have over a man. Fighting for control, she tried to pull away. He moaned in protest, his hands cupping her firm bottom, pulling her back to him.

His tongue probed again and again in a steady rhythm, sending waves of desire through her. It touched her everywhere, filling her with anticipation and more—a growing need. A need to cry out, to laugh, to move . . . or she'd burst. She broke away frantically, her hand catching in his shirt. Cotton ripped. Buttons flew.

Jeff's smile flashed as he shrugged off his shirt and glided toward her. "Hey, there, little wildcat, don't be in such a big hurry. We've got all night."

His strong arms reached out and pulled her up against his bare chest. Her fire-resistant shirt might have been paper, for all the protection it gave her. His heat seared through it into her breasts. Her body throbbed with the heat, matching the throbbing of his manhood, which was pressed against her again.

Suddenly she was frightened, not of Jeff but of herself. She had totally lost control of herself and the situation, and that had never happened before. Things were going too fast, much too fast.

"No," she said with a gasp. Pushing against his chest, she broke out of the circle of his arms. Hands raised, chest heaving, she glared at him. "Damn. Damn. Damn. Look what you've done." She called him names then, using all the curses Big Red had used and some she had made up.

Jeff stood, hands on hips, lips twitching. Finally, his easy drawl broke into her torrent. "I think the lady protests too much."

Unable to face his knowing grin she wheeled away, thumping and tripping her way through the trees to her equipment.

Jeff followed, watching as she kicked the silk parachute into a heap over a bed of moss.

"You're going to sleep out here?"

"You bet."

"Alone?"

Picking up the wet sleeping bag, she snapped it at him, then draped it over a low bush. "Damn right."

"Not afraid of wolves?"

"Only the two-legged kind."

He placed his hand on his bare chest, somewhere in the vicinity of his heart. "Ah, Li'l Red, you cut me."

"I'll do more than that if you come one step closer."

Jeff rocked back on his heels, studying her mournfully. "What a waste of a beautiful night. The moon's full. The air's warm . . . and full of love."

"And you're full of—"

He laughed. "You can't take a little teasing, can you?"

"Teasing! You're teasing?" She took a step toward him, wanting to throttle him, then stopped, thinking twice about getting too close. She contented herself with kicking an old cow pat at him. She missed. "How can you be teasing me at a time like this?"

"I've had lots of practice," Jeff said, thinking of his three sisters.

"I bet. Just because you're such a hot-shot Romeo doesn't mean you'll score with me."

"You're wrong about me, Caly," he said, raking his hand impatiently through his hair. "I'm not out to make a score."

"Then what are you trying to prove?" she muttered, kicking more dirt, but not at him.

He was silent for so long that Caly finally looked at him, wondering if he was going to answer.

"That you want to be a woman," he said softly.

She stamped her foot. "Well, I have news for you,

cowboy. Mount St. Helens will be stone cold long before I turn into a spineless, clinging woman."

He shook his head. "Ah, but you're mistaken, Li'l Red. Just because a woman is soft doesn't mean she's weak." He walked a few steps toward the cabin, then stopped and called back to her, "Think about it . . . while you lie there in your bed of silk."

Caly lay fully dressed, except for her boots, in her bed of silk. She was fuming.

All Mr. High-and-Mighty Jeff Adams wanted was to prove that she was soft. Simply because she almost had literally landed in his arms didn't mean she'd fall into his bed.

She didn't want his kisses, his caresses.

She didn't want those unknown feelings, longings.

No, dammit. She didn't want or need anything from this sexy cowboy.

Or did she?

Jeff sat on a log outside the cabin, watching with his good eye as the moonlight danced across the lake. The other eye, swollen shut, was aching.

Lord, did Caly ever pack a wallop—in more ways than one. She'd knocked down his fences and lassoed his heart, and all she'd done was hit him with her fist, then with her smile.

She was unlike any woman he'd ever known, and he had known a few in the seven years since Betsy had died. But he had never let another woman get close enough to touch his heart. He hadn't wanted to get involved again, hadn't wanted to take the risk of loving someone and losing her. So he'd remained aloof, despite the efforts of his family, friends, and fellow cowboys.

Until now.

Until a tomboy with red hair, freckles, and amber eyes had dropped out of the heavens and into his heart.

If he knew what was good for him, he'd stay as far from her as possible, but he couldn't seem to leave her alone. She fascinated him, attracted him, made him feel alive again.

Maybe he was feeling such strong emotions because he'd spent most of the day wondering what he was going to do with the rest of his life. He was thirty-five. It was high time he stopped mourning Betsy, found another wife, and raised a family. As much as he loved his sisters' kids, he wanted some of his own.

He needed a wife he could keep safe. And he could never keep Caly safe, he knew.

Loving Caly would bring nothing but trouble. She was exactly the opposite of the kind of wife he wanted, needed. She loved excitement, adventure, taking risks. She'd give him ulcers in no time flat. Either that or he'd try to change her, and he didn't think she'd take too kindly to change.

Maybe he wouldn't have to change her, he thought hopefully. He would be willing to bet his prize bull that somewhere under that tough tomboy exterior there was a woman ready for love. He'd caught glimpses of her, but he wondered if Caly even knew she existed.

Maybe, just maybe he could help her find that woman. And then . . .

No. It wouldn't work. She wasn't right for him.

But he could dream.

Three

Caly woke to the sound of chattering in the trees above her. A fir cone plopped on the silk beside her, and she grinned up at a sassy squirrel. A mountain blue jay trilled his joy with the new day, and, feeling the same anticipation, Caly got up and put on her boots.

After packing up the chutes and completing fifty push-ups, she was ready for a swim. Swinging her ditty bag over her shoulder, she strolled along the edge of the forest to the lake.

The sun hadn't reached the valley yet, but it bathed the nearby mountaintops in a rosy light. Blue smoke still hung in the trees. Despite the early-morning coolness, it was going to be another scorcher.

Removing her soap, towel, and clean panties from her bag, she felt a moment of regret that, because of her camera equipment, she had room only for essentials. She wished she had another change of clothes, but until now her cameras had been more important than her appearance.

Stripping off her clothes, she flipped them over a limb of a nearby tree. Unhooking the silver locket that nestled between her small, pert breasts, she hung it carefully on a broken branch and waded into the shallow lake. The water was so clear she could see her toes on the sandy bottom. But it was also freshly melted snow, and she flopped down quickly rather than prolonging the agony of getting wet.

Minutes later, body and hair clean, she started to wade to shore, but a curious otter swam by, and she joined him in a diving, splashing frolic. When he left abruptly, Caly rolled over onto her back and kicked her way leisurely toward the shore. An eagle whistled by at treetop level, and she stood up in waist-deep water to track its flight. The sun warmed her face and chest, but her lower body was rapidly becoming a block of ice. It was time to get out, she decided.

Turning, she spotted Jeff standing in the trees at the edge of the lake. From the expression on his face, Caly realized he'd been there for quite some time.

Embarrassed, she covered her breasts with her arms and sank into the water, knowing full well that her gesture was useless. The clear water wasn't going to hide her one little bit.

"Go away," she yelled, angry at being caught. She was mad at him and also mad at herself. Dammit, why had she fooled around so long? She should've known that he'd come looking for her as soon as he woke up. Why hadn't she had a quick wash and gotten dressed again?

Jeff approached the edge of the lake slowly. He had pulled on the blue shirt he'd worn the day before. Buttonless, it hung open, revealing a broad, muscular chest matted with black, curly hair. Her gaze dropped lower, then shot back up. His jeans were bulging in front.

She cursed herself silently, knowing who was responsible. Now what had she done? And what was he going to do? What was he thinking about? Why didn't he say something? The questions ran through her mind quickly.

Jeff stood still, gazing at her. Lord, she was beautiful, he thought, like a young fawn, shy but graceful. He knew that she was embarrassed, and almost wished he hadn't caught her bathing. Almost. He wouldn't have missed the sight of her standing in the water with the sun bathing her face and breasts for all the rain in Seattle.

A deep, aching longing swept through him. A longing so great, it made him forget for a brief moment the throbbing in his groin, but it demanded relief. Lord, he wanted her.

"Go away," she called again, breaking into his thoughts.

She watched as his white teeth flashed in a wicked smile. His black eye didn't help matters: He looked like a tousled, sexy rake.

"Why should I? I just came down for my morning swim." The duffel bag he dropped on a nearby log proved his quiet statement. "I can't help it if I find a mountain maiden in my swimming hole."

"You can leave till I'm finished bathing."

"Looks to me like you're all done bathing and are playing around." He stood at the water's edge, feet apart, his hands on his muscular thighs, smiling. "Shall I come in and play with you?"

Chills that had nothing to do with the glacial water ran down her spine.

"Now, listen here, you long-haired galoot, I'll blacken your other eye if you come near me," she sputtered bravely as she backed into deeper water.

He threw back his head and laughed, and she knew that she wouldn't stand a chance of blackening his other eye.

"You sure enough frighten me, Li'l Red, so I guess I'd better stay put until you come out." Backing up a step, he leaned against a fallen log and crossed his booted feet, giving every indication that he planned to stay there all day.

"I want to get out. Now."

"Nothing's stopping you, Li'l Red," he said in a drawl, rubbing his hand lazily over his bare chest.

She shivered, wishing fleetingly that his hand were warming her skin.

"You could at least turn your back."

"I'd much rather look at you."

"Jeff . . . it's freezing. I'm turning blue."

He yawned, stretching his arms up slowly, then dropping them to his sides. "I've always thought that red-headed women look best in blue."

She jogged in place, trying to warm up while remaining submerged. "J-J-Jeff . . ."

"Yes?"

"P-please turn your b-back while I get out."

"Well, since you've asked me real nice now, I guess I have to oblige you, Li'l Red." He swung his long legs over the log and faced the other way.

Caly splashed to shore and, picking up her towel, made two sketchy passes over her trembling body. She was trying to pull her panties up her still-damp legs when Jeff turned around and looked her over thoroughly.

Anchoring the towel on her chest with her chin, she glared at him as she attempted to dress behind the skimpy barrier.

"You lied. You promised to keep your back turned," she grumbled through clenched teeth, afraid to yell in case the towel dropped.

"Just until you got out of the water. I never said I wouldn't watch you dress."

"Some gentleman you are!"

His beautiful lips quirked. "Whatever gave you the idea I was a gentleman?"

"Cowboys are supposed to be knights of the range."

He laughed again. "You mean heroes in shining armor, and all that?"

"Right."

"Nope. At least this cowboy sure isn't." Leaning over, he pulled off one boot, then the other. Brown socks followed.

"What are you doing?" Caly eyed him warily as she stepped into her baggy pants.

"Taking my swim. Any objections?" Rising to his feet, he shrugged out of his shirt, then began unbuckling his belt.

"You could at least wait until I leave." She pulled on her yellow shirt, fumbling with the buttons, then dropped the towel.

"If I waited any longer, Li'l Red, I'd burst." He edged the zipper down carefully. "Sure wish you'd change your mind and join me." He wore navy briefs. "We could have ourselves quite a time."

She didn't have to guess at what he was talking about. It was very evident. Hooking her locket off the tree, she snatched up her boots and bag and fled.

"You're not going to stay?" he called after her. "I'm crushed. I thought you'd at least want to watch."

Caly heard the laughter in his voice. For a moment she was tempted to call his bluff, then thought better of it. He'd probably go right ahead and parade around naked, and she'd be the one with the red face. Not he.

When Jeff strolled into the cabin half an hour later, Caly was standing at the table dishing up breakfast from a heavy cast-iron frying pan. She glared at him, trying not to notice how handsome he looked in his clean blue shirt. Reluctant to face him yet, Caly returned to the stove with the empty frying pan.

She looked so cute and so indignant that Jeff couldn't let her get away with ignoring him. Sneaking across the room, he bent over and nuzzled her neck.

"Hmm, you smell good," he murmured.

"What the—" Whirling around, she dropped the frying pan. It hit his big toe and bounced, splattering grease on his boot, then rolled onto the floor.

"Ouch!" Jeff leaped backward. Jumping to retrieve the pan, Caly slipped on the grease and rammed into Jeff.

"I'm—I'm—t-terribly s-sorry." Appalled by what she'd done, she stood with her head down, watching grease drip from the frying pan onto his other boot.

"What do you . . . do for encores?" he asked.

Caly decided that she wasn't totally responsible for the fiasco. "Me!" Her eyes flashed at him. "It was all your fault." She waved the frying pan in his direction. "You were the one who sneaked up on me."

"Okay, okay." Holding up his hands in surrender, he backed away. "I should know by now that a man risks life and limb if he gets too close to you."

"You can't say I didn't warn you."

He tried a weak smile. "You should be posted with a sign saying, 'Danger! Keep away.' " He turned toward the table. "Let's eat while I can still chew."

Placing the frying pan on the back of the stove, Caly carefully poured the coffee and sat down at the table. Jeff eyed his bacon and eggs doubtfully, and she really didn't blame him. The bacon was raw in the places where it wasn't burnt, and the eggs were watery.

"I told you I wasn't a very good cook," she mumbled.

She was aware that he wasn't eating, and after a few minutes she raised her eyes and found him looking at her. There was something in his face—desire, maybe—but it was quickly replaced with a roguish grin.

"And I see that you don't believe in sewing on buttons either," His voice was soft, suggestive.

Glancing down, Caly saw that her shirt was open, exposing enough of her breasts that she could see the locket that nestled between them. Ears burning, she realized she'd been so flustered at the lake, she hadn't fastened the safety pin she was using to replace the lost top button. Her recent exertion with the frying pan had pulled the next button open too.

"Don't bother on my account. I like the view," he said teasingly as she hastily refastened the button and safety pin.

"A . . . a gentleman wouldn't have looked."

"I told you before, I'm no gentleman." His green eye sparkled. He shoved his eggs around on the plate, then, with a sigh, forked them into his mouth and swallowed quickly.

She followed suit, demolishing her breakfast with a couple of gulps. "I don't know why all this is happening," she said, wiggling on her stump.

"You mean you aren't this clumsy around other men?" he asked, looking at her over the brim of his cup as he drained the last of his coffee.

"Hell, no. And I'm around them constantly." She clinked her fork against the edge of her plate.

She looked so embarrassed that he didn't dare laugh. "Hmm."

"So it must be all your fault."

"My fault?"

"Well, you shouldn't sneak up behind a person like that." She shook her fork at him; then, realizing what she was doing, she dropped it on the table. "You're liable to get killed," she muttered.

Pushing his plate aside, he reached across the table and picked up her hand, holding it loosely. "Look, Li'l Red. Seeing as how it's my fault that we got off on the wrong foot, or eye, so to speak"—his good eye twinkled—"and because this happens to be the last clean shirt I have with me . . . ." He squeezed her hand briefly. "Why don't we both calm down?"

"Deal." She beamed at him, shaking his hand in a bone-crushing grip. Suddenly she let go and moved her hand carefully to her side. With her luck she'd knock over the coffeepot or do something else equally dumb, she thought. He made her so nervous. How could she stop being such a klutz around him?

Leaning back on his stump, Jeff raised his arms in a slow, careful stretch, then rolled his shoulders, loosening his tense muscles.

"Guess I'd better get to work. Would you like to come with me? I've got to pack some salt blocks up the mountain."

Rising, he sauntered to the door, hooking his Stetson off the wall peg on his way.

Caly followed him outside and stood looking back and forth between the meadow and the mountains. Sensing her indecision, Jeff reached out and ruffled her hair. "You don't have to, you know." Holding a curl between two long fingers, he twisted it back and forth, watching the way the sun turned it into a flame.

She reached up to remove his hand but was halted by the soft look in his eye. Caught under his spell, she swayed closer. His hand moved to her cheek, and he lowered his head slowly. She licked her lips nervously, wanting him to kiss her. But it would be too dangerous, she told herself. Abruptly she backed out of his reach. He let her go, giving her a lopsided smile. His green eye sparkled again, reminding her of sunlight on Emerald Lake. Sunlight sparkled through her, too, making her want to melt.

What had they been talking about, anyway? she wondered. Oh, yes, whether or not she'd go riding with him. She wanted to, but the way she was feeling, she'd be asking for trouble.

"What I'd really like to do is stay here and take pictures," Caly said, her expression daring him to call her a liar. It hadn't been a lie moments before. When she'd stepped out of the cabin, all she'd wanted to do was to spend the day taking pictures—and, more important, restoring her soul with the beauty around her.

"Pictures? What kind of pictures?"

"Photos. You know, the kind you take with a camera." She looked at him through the frame of her fingers and snapped an imaginary shutter.

"You mean you're a professional photographer too?"

"No. It's just a hobby."

She sounded very convincing, but something told him that she was more talented than she let on. Normally he'd have staked his herd on his instincts, but in her case it might have been wishful thinking.

"What are you going to take pictures of?" he asked, glancing around.

"Lots of things. The lupines under the trees." She pointed to the purple carpet beneath the green pines. "And the spring beauties," she continued, waving a hand at the mass of tiny white flowers that nestled shyly in the grass at her feet.

"Is that what they're called?"

"Aren't they beautiful?" she asked, kneeling in the grass and lifting one with her fingertip.

Jeff squatted beside her. "They aren't the only beautiful thing," he said huskily, leaning over to brush a kiss on her cheek.

Startled, Caly jerked forward. Jeff caught her to him, laughing as he fell backward in the grass. Rolling over on top of her, he lowered his head.

"I've been wanting to do this all morning," he said as his lips covered hers.

Her mouth tasted of clover and honey—so sweet, so pure, so good. He savored her slowly, thoroughly, drinking nectar from her velvet depths, wanting to taste all of her. Leaving her lips, he nibbled his way to the sensitive cord under her ear, feeling her shuddering response under him. Spurred on by her reaction and his own need, his lips sought the opening in her shirt that had beckoned during breakfast. Her breasts were as soft as he'd imagined, and he kissed his way down the sweet valley to the locket. He wanted to do more than kiss her. He wanted her completely, and the way her heart was pounding, he knew she wouldn't put up much of a fight.

But he also knew it wasn't right.

Slowly he lifted his head and looked down into her eyes. They were wide open. She appeared dazed and very vulnerable. She might have let him make love to her then, but she'd probably have regretted it afterward. He'd have to move carefully or he'd hurt her. Lord, it was going to be hard, he thought.

He brushed a lock of hair off her forehead, then ran his fingers through her mass of curls, lifting them to catch the sunlight again.

"It's as if I'm holding fire in my hands," he said hoarsely, trying to control the feelings that threatened to rip him apart.

She stared at him, eyes wide.

"And your eyes are the color of sunshine on autumn tamaracks. My favorite color."

Copper lashes covered her eyes, then flew open as he ran a finger along the side of her jaw and into the sweet curve of her neck. "And the freckle fairy was so very generous with her kisses." He kissed a few of the freckles, ending with one on the tip of her nose. "Such a cute little nose."

In the meadow a calf bellowed and a cow answered, reminding him that he had a job to do. Sighing, he raised his head and looked down into her shining eyes. "Someday I'd like to kiss every one of them, but I've gotta get to work. It sure is hard to get anything done with such an enticing woman around to distract me."

"I didn't entice you," she said breathlessly, a smile trembling on her kiss-swollen lips.

"Oh, yes, you did, Li'l Red. It's all your fault I'm lying in the grass wasting my time." He dropped another kiss on her nose. "You made me stop and look at the wild flowers. It's the first time I've done that in years. Since I was a kid, in fact."

With one lithe move he was on his feet and walking toward the corral singing, "Oh, What a Beautiful Morning" perfectly in tune.

Dazed by her emotions, Caly sat in the grass watching as he saddled Buck, loaded pink-and-white blocks of salt on the other two horses, and rode away, waving his wide-brimmed black Stetson.

What was happening to her? She'd never felt that way before.

It was a long time before Caly pulled the Minolta X700 and the macro zoom lens out of her bag and went looking for her first subject. Between dreaming of Jeff and taking pictures, the day passed quickly. She took her time with each of the flower pictures, picking the perfect specimen, arranging the background, and waiting for the exact combination of light and shadow. Often, when she was photographing, she'd wait for hours and still not get the right conditions, but this time she was lucky. She had stumbled onto a patch of Avalanche lilies, their yellow heads nodding so close together that they made the meadow sparkle with gold.

She barely was conscious of the nose-tingling smell of the pines or the wind whirring in the treetops or the slippery silk of the long, dry needles underfoot as she walked from one shot to the next.

As the hours passed, peace replaced exhaustion, and joy returned. It had been ages since she'd had the time to really take pictures, ones that she knew would satisfy her demanding standards. And it had been a long time between her "beauty treatments" too. She smiled as she thought how ridiculous the phrase would sound to other women. They went to the beauty parlor when they wanted to feel good. She went to the forest.

In the late afternoon she came across a black bear, and after they struck up a nodding acquaintance, she followed it deeper into the woods. Sure enough, a cub was there, and she snapped pictures with delight.

A crashing in the underbrush startled them, and three pairs of eyes looked to the opening where Jeff sat on his horse, pointing a rifle at the bear. Automatically Caly snapped a picture, then lowered her camera and realized how grim his expression was.

"Don't shoot," Caly called, suddenly aware of the danger he presented.

"I won't unless she charges. Back toward me slowly."

Realizing that it would be dangerous to argue, Caly did as she was told, and was hauled up behind Jeff by the waist of her pants. Mother bear watched them anxiously as Jeff whirled Buck around and guided him through the trees.

Clutching her precious camera in one hand, Caly wrapped the other arm around Jeff's waist, holding him tightly. She didn't have to hang on, but she liked the feel of his solid body against her. He smelled of sweat, horses, and cattle—good, honest, hard-working smells. She pressed closer.

Once they were out of danger, Jeff slowed Buck to a walk, then gave her a furious look over his shoulder.

"I turn my back for a few hours, and you go and pull a dumb, greenhorn stunt. I thought you knew your way around the woods."

"I was doing very well without your help," Caly pointed out mildly, rubbing her chin against his shoulder.

"Doing well! You were taking pictures of a cub while the mother bear breathed down your neck."

"It wasn't quite like that."

"You could've been killed."

Caly barely heard his words. She was much more conscious of her breasts rubbing against Jeff's supple body. Her nipples hardened, then throbbed as she and Jeff swayed in rhythm with the horse. Rivers of heat flowed through her, to gather where her thighs pressed against the saddle. The movement of the horse under her made her very aware of the lower part of her body. She wanted to ride forever and ever with her Virginian and keep feeling these stimulating sensations, but all too soon he reined up beside the corral, threw his leg over the saddle horn, and stepped down, leaving her with one big ache.

She slid reluctantly to the ground, and he caught her arm to steady her. Releasing it, he sheathed the rifle, then led Buck into the corral. Still bemused, she watched Jeff as he unsaddled Buck and fed the horses. By the time he'd finished his chores, an irresistible urge to live dangerously had taken hold of Caly, making her want to see how far she could provoke Jeff, and what would happen if he lost control.

"Have you stopped being scared yet?" she asked, placing her camera on a bag of feed nearby.

"Scared?" He swung over the top rail and planted himself in front of her.

"Yes, scared."

Before she could move he shackled her wrists in his hands.

"Damn right, I was scared." He glared down at her in exasperation. "For you."

His expression softened. She melted. No one had ever looked at her with so much concern before.

"I'm sorry I frightened you," she whispered. "But you don't have to worry about me around wild animals—or any other animal, for that matter. I have . . . a gift . . . I guess you could say. Animals trust me."

"What about that bull?" He shook his head in disbelief, his hands dropping away.

Her eyes were the color of maple syrup as she smiled at him. "He was the exception."

"So you didn't need rescuing this time?" He touched the tip of her nose with a finger that still trembled.

"Nope. I enjoyed it, though." She smiled at him saucily. "And I really should thank you for rescuing me."

He stepped forward. "How?"

With no thought of the consequences, Caly snaked her arms around his neck, stood on her toes, and kissed him—hard. She strained against him, working her hands up the back of his head. His hat landed in the dust at their feet.

Lord. He'd been thinking about her kiss all day. It was heaven, pure heaven. She kissed like an angel. Like a wildcat. He was lost. His hand slid down her back, pressing her into the fork of his thighs. He felt an immediate surge in his loins. He was in a bad way. He held her there as long as he could stand it, then eased her away. Things were too damn tight. With a groan, he broke free from her lips and bent to fumble with his chaps.

As he loosened the straps, Caly nuzzled the base of his throat, tasting the salt, feeling the heat of his skin. Her breasts brushed against his muscular chest as she reached up to touch his blackened eye with her lips. He held still while she kissed his eye again and again.

"Ah, Caly, Caly, what you do to me," he said, his arms circling her.

Since she was clasped tightly to his hard body, her nipples became sensitive to the slightest pressure. She arched against him, feeling an aching in her breasts, a throbbing, a desire that left her hot. Easing back a bit, she smiled up at Jeff, seeing her desire mirrored in his face.

The top button of his shirt was open, and she wound one hand through his wiry hair while the fingers of her other hand traced the curve of his lips. Then her mouth covered his, and she drank from his well of passion as if she were dying of thirst. Her thirst wasn't sated, and she demanded more, seeking and gaining entry. He groaned. His body quivered. His hand caught the back of her head, pushing her closer. Heedless of the consequences, she foraged further, probing him with the same rhythm that he had used earlier. She pressed her pelvis against his throbbing hardness and felt the heat burning between them.

Without knowing how it happened, she was on her back on the ground, with Jeff on top. She welcomed his weight, reveled in her power. Raising up on his elbows, he leaned over her, his eyes glazed, his breathing labored. A sheen of perspiration covered his forehead.

"I want you, Betsy," he said, groaning in desperation.

She wanted him, too, and lifted her pelvis eagerly to meet him.

Then it hit her. Betsy! He had called her Betsy. Jeff didn't want her; he wanted someone else.

Four

"Get off me." Angrily Caly struck out at him, twisting and turning.

Surprised, he rolled onto his side and lay there breathing heavily.

"What the devil's going on?"

Scrambling to her feet, she glared down at him "I don't want to make love." She lied. Her body ached with passion, but she didn't want to make love with Jeff if he considered her just a substitute for another woman.

He pounded the earth with a clenched fist, then elbowed himself into a sitting position. "Doggone it, Caly. Do you know what you've done to me?" He slapped the ground again. "What kind of game are you playing?"

"Game! I'm not the one playing games. You called me Betsy," she cried, kicking at a piece of deadfall, wishing it were Jeff. It exploded with a dull crack.

He stared at her in dismay. "Betsy? I called you Betsy?"

"Yes," she said, fighting to stem the torrent of curses she wanted to scream at him. Never had she felt so hurt or so betrayed.

"Hell!" Propping his elbows on his bent knees, he buried his face in his hands. "I'm sorry, Caly."

"I won't be a substitute for another woman. You can damn well wait till you get home."

He rubbed his face wearily, then let his hands hang loosely between his knees. "There's no other woman."

"Hah!" Caly's next kick sent his hat sailing.

"It's true. Betsy was my wife."

"What?" she asked, staring at him. His head was bowed, his shoulders hunched.

"Betsy was my wife," he repeated softly.

The pain in his voice made her almost afraid to ask the question that burned in her mind. "Was?"

"She died. Seven years ago."

She was stunned. Jeff was too young to be a widower.

She sank to her knees beside him, placing a hand on his shoulder. "I'm sorry, Jeff." He kept his head bowed, but did nothing to stop her hand as she rubbed soothingly.

They sat in silence. He knew he should tell her that Betsy had died in a barrel-race accident, but it didn't seem to be the right time.

Caly watched the thunder clouds pile over the mountains, wondering about Betsy and about the man who still loved her after so many years.

"You must have loved her very much."

"She was always my sweetheart." Raising his head, he smiled at her, making no effort to hide his feelings. "But it's time to let her go."

Caly was confused by the vulnerability and love she saw in his face. No man had ever looked at her like that before, but was he thinking about Betsy or her? Suddenly she needed to move, to get away from this cowboy who was overwhelming her. As she got to her feet, he also did so. Placing a hand on her shoulder, he turned her toward him.

"Wait, Caly. I want to explain. There's no excuse for

what happened . . . but I've been thinking about Betsy a lot today . . . and about you . . ."

She blinked and lowered her eyes.

"What about me?"

He brushed his thumb tenderly across her jaw, then tilted her chin up. "For the first time since Betsy died, I've met a woman who's made me feel alive," he said, his voice caressing her.

She stared at him, wanting to believe him, but when he lowered his head to kiss her, she turned away ever so slightly.

Her movement was enough to tell Jeff that the moment was gone. With a sigh he dropped his hand to his side, wondering if he'd get another chance to make amends.

Thunder rumbled, and Jeff glanced toward the mountains. A towering ridge of white clouds, with rapidly blackening bottoms, obscured the peaks.

"Looks as if we're in for a storm."

Caly assessed the clouds briefly. "Just lightning, I'm afraid."

After climbing into the corral, Jeff retrieved his Stetson, reshaped it, and clapped it on the back of his head. He picked up her camera and studied it carefully. "This is top of the line, isn't it?" he asked, handing it to her.

"Mmm." Caly readied the camera quickly, then swung it up and snapped his picture. Silhouetted against the white-and-black thunder clouds, he looked wild, rugged, untamed.

"What the—" he asked, startled, his hand going self-consciously to his black eye.

"Hope you don't mind if I take your picture now and then. I need the practice."

"I thought you weren't serious about photography."

"I'm not. It's just a hobby." The defensive tone in her voice made Jeff doubt her even more.

"Would you show me your photos sometime?"

"Sure," she agreed, before she realized what was involved. All her photographs were in her cabin at Emerald Lake, and she didn't think they'd every be going there together.

"I'll hold you to that."

He kept his arm around her shoulders as they walked to the cabin. She moved gracefully, her long legs carrying her easily across the uneven ground. His body stirred as he remembered how beautiful she'd looked earlier in the morning, standing in the lake. Damn, he was in a bad way. He had been all day.

Entering the cabin, Caly stopped dead and stared dumbfounded at the two Calypso orchids that stood in a jelly jar in the center of the table.

"Oh, Jeff!" she said, moving across the room almost in a trance. With a trembling finger she traced the pink throat of the delicate orchid. She blinked back unexpected tears, hoping that Jeff wouldn't notice them. For some unknown reason she felt like crying, and that was something she never did. "Where did you find them?"

He stood beside her, watching her. "They were hiding. They reminded me of you." He touched her hair lightly, then dropped his hand to his side. "Beautiful, but shy."

From deep inside surged an overwhelming longing to be beautiful, to be loved by this cowboy, to love this cowboy with all her heart and soul. She blew out a long breath of air, fighting down the panic that followed quickly on the heels of her longing. She couldn't love Jeff.

Slowly she raised her head and looked at him. He smiled at her, searching her flushed face.

"They are me," she said, hoping he wouldn't guess what she'd been thinking. "I mean, I was named after them."

"Caly?"

"No, Calypso. They're Calypso orchids." A smile trembled on her lips. "Thank you for bringing them to me."

He ducked his head and shuffled his feet, and Caly realized that her Virginian was one embarrassed cowboy.

"Sit down, will you," he said gruffly, walking to the stove. "I'll cook supper."

"You don't want me to cook?" she asked teasingly, trying to relieve her own tension as well as his embarrassment.

"You're darn tootin'. We don't have any food to waste, and my body is a mass of bruises," he answered with a laugh.

They joked and laughed through the entire meal, and Caly enjoyed every mouthful.

"Are you sure you aren't a gourmet cook?"

"Lord, no, but I do all right when I have to."

"If I'd known you had this steak, I would've insisted on putting it on your eye."

"What, and ruin a perfectly good piece of meat? I'd much rather eat it than wear it, thank you."

They had just finished cleaning up when the first crash of thunder shook the sod roof. It was followed immediately by another deafening crack. The storm had arrived with a vengeance.

Caly walked slowly to the open cabin door and stared out at the threatening sky. She hated lightning storms, especially dry lightning storms, because they were so destructive. Without rain to quench the tongues of flame, the resultant fires would ravage the forest.

She wrapped her arms around her middle, feeling sick. Then Jeff was there, holding her in his arms. She leaned against him, feeling safe and sheltered as they watched nature's fireworks. White streaks of light sizzled in the air, the wind screamed through the trees, and the heavens boomed.

Gradually the fury passed over, and Caly started to breathe normally again. Then suddenly a blue-white bolt of lightning speared toward them, and flames engulfed a tall pine at the far end of the lake.

Instantly Caly was out the door, running in the direction of the corral.

"Come on," she yelled over her shoulder. "That strike will take off if we don't stop it."

Already the wind was fanning the fire, pushing it through the underbrush and up the mountain. As soon as it built up enough heat, it would flash into the treetops, and there'd be no stopping it.

Jeff grasped her arm as she picked up the Pulaski. "Let it burn."

She pulled away impatiently. "No. We have to fight it. *Now!*" The wind whipped her curls around her head.

"I don't want you to fight it. Leave it alone." He reached for her again. She brushed his hand away angrily.

"What's the matter? Are you afraid?" Her voice dripped sarcasm.

"Hell no, its just—"

"Look, cowboy, there's no time to argue," she broke in. "If you're coming, come on. If not, get out of my way." Juggling the Pulaski and water pack, she reached for the rest of the equipment.

Pushing her aside, Jeff grabbed the shovel and crosscut saw. "You're the boss. Lead on."

Catching a glimpse of his angry face, Caly knew a moment of fear. Now she'd gone and done it. She'd called him a coward, and she doubted if anyone ever got away with that. She would pay for her remarks later, but she couldn't worry about it just then. They had a fire to fight.

The cattle had taken shelter in the woods, so she led the way straight across the meadow and around the far end of the lake. Climbing above the fire, they began digging a fire line. Using the hoe part of the Pulaski, Caly grubbed down to rock while Jeff shoveled the fuel away from the approaching flames. Smoke swirled around them, choking them, blinding them. Underbrush crackled, then roared as it ignited. The flames leaped higher; the heat grew more intense. It was a battle, but they won the first skirmish, completing the trench around the hottest part of the fire before it broke through.

To better their odds, Caly started a backfire. A limb crashed beside her, and, jumping backward to avoid it, she tripped on a rock and fell. Jeff appeared out of the swirling smoke and hauled her to her feet.

"Are you okay?" he asked, pulling her against him. His chest heaved and his body trembled, and he held her as if he'd never let her go.

"Yeah. Sure." She rested a moment, wanting to stay in his arms. But they still had a fire to fight, she realized. Breaking out of his grip, she backed away. Needing something to do with her hands, she brushed them down her pants and found a large rip in the back. She smiled at Jeff, hoping to ease the strain she saw on his face.

"D'ya think Garfield iron-on patches will work on this?" Turning around, she wagged the flap of cloth back and forth with her hand, and was rewarded with a snort.

"Nope."

"Me neither. Sure hope you have an extra pair of jeans."

He caught her shoulder and gazed down at her in concern. "Take a break, Caly."

She shook her head. "Can't. Gotta see if this backfire will work." She swung around to look at the fire line. "Good thing the wind's died down. We might have a chance if we ring it back to the lake."

Without another word, Jeff picked up the Pulaski. During the rest of the long night, Caly thought of nothing but Jeff. She was pleased with how well they worked together. When she told him what to do, he did it, no questions asked. And he worked hard, taking the heavy end of the crosscut saw and hauling most of the water up the steep mountain slope.

She was sorry she had called him a coward. He definitely was not a coward. He certainly had earned her admiration and respect.

Working beside her, Jeff was amazed by her determination. She fought the fire as if it were a mortal enemy. More than once he heard her cursing it, threatening it, telling it that she would beat it no matter what.

He didn't know where she found the breath to talk. He had none. His lungs were full of smoke and ached from the effort of breathing. His throat was raw and burning, and his eyes—even the swollen one—felt as though they were seared. The intense heat seemed to suck every drop of moisture out of his body.

As he hacked and scrapped, all he could think was, thank heaven Caly wouldn't have to fight another fire. They'd get married right away and she could quit. Thank heaven he could keep her safe.

The morning sun had cleared the mountain before Caly felt it was safe to leave the burn. Leading the way, she stumbled along the edge of the lake to the place where they had swum the day before. The wind had been blowing in the other direction, and very little fire debris marred the calm surface of the water. Kneeling beside it, they drank slowly, deeply, then stretched out in the thick grass.

"What I wouldn't give for a tall gin and tonic. And I don't even like gin," Jeff said hoarsely.

Caly propped herself up on an elbow and smiled down at him. Ashes clung to his damp curls. Both his eyes were red rimmed and watering. His face was grimy with soot and streaked with tears—and he was so handsome, he made her want to cry.

"I can't do anything about the gin and tonic, but I can fix up something that'll make you feel better. Do you have any potatoes?"

"There are a few in the box in the cabin," He coughed. "Why? You're not going to cook breakfast, are you?"

She smiled at his tone of disbelief. "Nope. Stay put. I'll be back."

She returned a few minutes later and, kneeling beside him, placed a poultice of grated potatoes over his closed eyes.

"What's that?" he asked, startled. Reaching up he fingered the old cotton dishcloth she had used to wrap the potatoes in.

"Just something to relieve the burning," she reassured him as she lay down beside him and covered her eyes with a second poultice.

"Thanks," he mumbled. After a bit he added, "It does feel better." He coughed harshly, then centered the poultice again. "I didn't know a person could eat so much smoke and survive."

She laughed hoarsely. "That's why they call us smoke-eaters."

"I'm sure as hell glad I don't do this for a living."

"You were terrific." A tension hung between them, and she knew it was time to make her apologies. "I want to thank you for your help, Jeff," she said. "And to tell you I'm sorry that I called you a coward."

For a moment she thought he wasn't going to accept her apology, and realized just how much she had hurt him with her thoughtless words.

"That's okay," he said, finally.

"No, it isn't. You definitely aren't a coward, so you must've had a good reason for not wanting to fight the fire." She left it as a question that he could answer if he wished.

Jeff didn't know if he wanted to explain, but Caly was whistling again, a gasping, tuneless whistle that left little doubt how upset she was.

He cleared his throat. "I didn't want you to fight that fire," he said in a husky voice. "And I thought that if I didn't go, you wouldn't go either."

"But it's my job to fight fires. We've been through this before."

"I know. I know. I just wanted to protect you."

"I don't need your protection, Jeff." She realized how rude she sounded, but it was the truth. "But thanks for your help. We made a good team, didn't we?"

"We sure did. You're one hell of a fire fighter, Caly." There was admiration in his voice, and something else, which sounded like resignation. "You fight a fire as if it's a living thing. It doesn't matter how big or how small it is, you need to destroy it, don't you?"

His insight surprised her. None of the other men she'd worked with had guessed how she felt about fighting fires.

"Yeah," she said slowly, heavily.

"Why?"

"Because fire destroys so much." She knew she should tell Jeff about her parents, but she couldn't just yet.

After a few moments, Jeff spoke again, his voice thoughtful. "I'm sure you'd be the first to admit that a forest needs fire as well as water before it can grow." He raised himself up, coughed, then thumped some more smoke out of his chest before lying back and replacing the poultice. "The forests shouldn't be overprotected."

She gave a short laugh. "You're right. And people are the same. They shouldn't be overprotected either."

He heard the warning in her words and knew that it was aimed at him. But he couldn't help how he felt. He wanted—no, needed—to protect her, and he knew she wouldn't stand for it.

"Guess you're right," he muttered.

She felt the tension in him, and when his fingers touched hers cautiously, she let him take her hand. His grip was firm but gentle.

She lay there in silence, letting the heat of the sun soak into her aching muscles. The forest was alive with the chirping of birds, and in the meadow a calf bellowed for its mother.

"Anyway, thank you for not arguing every time I gave you an order, the way some of the men I work with do." After a moment she asked, "I wonder why?"

The ball of his thumb traced slow circles in the palm of her hand. "Probably because they don't feel secure enough about themselves as men to let a woman boss them around."

Thinking about the men she'd worked with in the past, remembering the ones who had taken her orders and those who had fought her every step of the way, she realized that what Jeff said made sense. And she also realized why he was so special. He knew who he was, and therefore didn't have to prove himself.

"Thank heaven you're not that way."

"Has it been hard for you, being a woman in a man's world?"

"Sometimes. What makes me so mad is when people insinuate that I got the job with the Smokejumpers because they needed a token woman." Her voice broke, and she coughed harshly. "Token woman, my foot! I'm in better shape than a lot of the men, and I can hold my own with any of them on the fire line." Over half of the recruits washed out during training camp, and she was proud of the fact that she had been one of the top Smokejumpers in her group.

"And that makes you happy?"

"Yes."

"That's sad," Jeff said quietly, realizing she had been so busy being tough all her life that she hadn't had a chance to be soft.

Caly didn't know what he meant but was too tired to ask. And when Jeff leaned over and kissed her nose, she was so exhausted, she couldn't open her eyes.

"Caly."

"Hmm."

"Let's clean up and go to bed."

"Too tired. Just let me stay here for a while."

"If you lie here any longer, you won't move."

"Hmm."

"Sleep, then, and leave everything to me."

Floating on a plane somewhere between total exhaustion and unconsciousness, Caly was aware that Jeff left her . . . returned . . . removed her clothes and boots, and carried her into the lake.

The cold water shocked her and made her aware of his hands soaping her body quickly, thoroughly but gently; of his naked leg, which supported her; of the fact that she felt safe and secure. Just before sleep claimed her again, she realized that, for the first time since she was seven, she trusted another person besides Big Red.

Jeff looked down at the woman who lay in his arms. His good eye still burned, and tears blurred his vision.

But he could feel the hard muscles of her arms and legs, the softness of her skin, her fine bones. She was so thin, so fragile.

Lord, he couldn't bear to see one of her copper hairs singed or one of her freckles bruised. And if she were badly burned . . . or killed—

He wouldn't think about it.

From deep inside him rose the overwhelming need to protect her, to keep her safe from all harm, to cherish her. And above all else, to love her.

The hot sun woke Caly. She stretched, feeling something silky and sensuous under her. Remembering the fire, she sat up quickly and looked at the mountain. Only a few trails of gray smoke lingered in the trees. Relieved, she settled back, then realized she was lying on her silk parachute—and she was naked.

Languorous warmth flooded through her as she remembered how Jeff had bathed her, wrapped her in a towel, and had eased her into her bed of silk. The towel was now covering her hips.

The man beside her stirred in his sleep. He lay on his stomach, facing away from her, his head buried in the red-and-white silk. Outside of the towel draped over one leg, he, too, was naked.

She sat up again, ready to flee, then realized she didn't want to. She wanted to stay and look at Jeff.

He was tanned all over, except for the area that would have been covered by a bathing suit. Curly black hair covered his back. Muscles rippled in a smooth sweep from his broad shoulders across his flat buttocks and down powerful legs to his feet. Even in sleep he looked lethal, like a deadly cougar.

Drawn by an irresistible urge, she reached out and ran a finger down the valley between his shoulders. He grunted, hunching his shoulders backward, then he relaxed.

Smiling, she stroked him again.

Lifting his head, he turned toward her and looked at her sleepily from under his long, thick lashes.

"So, the little wildcat wants to play," he said with a growl, his good eye widening in appreciation as it roamed over her body.

The glint in his eye made Caly remember that she was naked. She grabbed for her towel, but he swept it out of reach with a quick flick of his hand.

"Oh, no, you don't. It's my turn to look," he said in a lazy drawl.

She sank back on the silk, attempting to cover herself with her hands.

Turning on his side, he smiled down at her.

"Don't do that, honey. Don't be ashamed of your body. You're beautiful."

"I'm not beautiful."

"Oh, but you are."

"My breasts are too small." She said the first thing that came to her mind.

He inspected them carefully, and rather than feeling offended by his gaze, Caly felt her breasts swell and tingle. "They're perfect. All a man could ask for."

Jeff lowered his head, touching one pouting peak with his lips, then moving to the other. Soon they no longer pouted, but stood erect, begging for attention. He gave it freely, rolling a nipple between his lips, then nipping it gently, then sucking it with an urgency that took her breath away.

"Jeff," she whispered in protest, but as the warmth coursed through her body, her words of demur became purrs of contentment. "That feels so good."

"Where? Tell me." He raised his head and smiled at her so tenderly that Caly didn't even think about being embarrassed, either by his words or by her feelings.

"Here." She cupped her hands around her breasts, trying to hold their fullness. He nuzzled his face between them. Caly squirmed under his caresses, wanting to escape the sweet erotic torture of his touch—but not wanting to miss it either.

She had no reason to be afraid of Jeff. Hadn't he bathed her and lain with her when she'd been too exhausted to move—or to resist him if he had tried to make love?

She was awake now, and she wanted him to make love to her. In less than forty-eight hours she had changed from a tomboy who knew nothing about her own body, into a woman who ached for a man. But it wasn't just any man she wanted to love her. She wanted only Jeff. He was right for her, and she trusted him.

He slid his hand down her body to the mound of hair that covered her womanhood, moving it in a rolling motion that sent a series of shock waves through her. When his fingers found their way into her soft flesh, she didn't protest, couldn't protest. She wanted to feel him there.

"Jeff, teach me to be a woman, please," she whispered breathlessly.

He raised his head and smiled down at her.

"Are you sure, Caly?"

She gazed back at him with imploring eyes. "With you, yes."

"How does this feel? Tell me," he demanded lovingly again as he stroked her slowly.

"Good. Soooo good."

"Slower?" His fingers teased.

"No. Faster."

His lips claimed hers, and his tongue slipped easily past all barriers, filling her warmth completely. He waited for a moment, then began probing her mouth in slow, steady strokes, capturing her, making her his.

She arched against his hand, not wanting him to stop until she had experienced everything.

"Ummm, yes," she said.

"Does that feel good?" he murmured against her lips.

"Yes. Don't stop," she pleaded, concentrating on the feelings in the core of her being. The pool of molten lava ebbed back and forth until it erupted into waves of heat that swept through her, one after another. Then, when she thought she couldn't stand it a moment longer, the core blew out of her center, making her heave and tremble with pleasure.

Jeff watched as expressions of excitement, wonder, and passion chased across her face.

"My Lord," Jeff said, breathing heavily. "You're so beautiful, Caly. So responsive. So desirable."

She opened her eyes and saw him above her, his face filled with happiness for her.

She quivered, feeling like warm honey and melted butter.

He stretched out beside her, his body cool against her heat.

"I didn't know it was possible for a man to make a woman feel that way without . . . you know . . . really making love," she whispered, moving against him sensuously. His skin felt like a chamois, and his body hair tantalized her. Something else tantalized and tempted her, something very hard. "But what about you? You haven't . . . you know," she said hesitantly.

Jeff laughed softly. "I'll survive."

"But that's not fair. I want you to be satisfied too." She threaded her fingers through the mat of hair on his chest. It was thick and curly and springy—stimulating, sexy.

He lifted his head and looked into her eyes. "Are you sure, Caly?"

"Very sure." Her eyes smoldered with a new sexual awareness. "Why are you being so noble?"

She rubbed her body against him. Jeff ignited like dry tinder.

"Damned if I know."

Rolling onto his back, he pulled her hands down his hard stomach, just above that part of him that he could no longer ignore.

"Touch me," he said hoarsely.

Taking him at his word, she moved her hands boldly through the wiry hair that covered his pelvis and encircled the throbbing root that lay below. It vibrated with life.

He sucked in his breath as a shudder swept through him.

"That feels so good."

"This?"

She moved her hand again, stroking him lightly.

"Hmm."

As she caressed and explored, his body trembled, and he grew hotter, thicker, heavier. She also trembled, growing warmer, wetter, sexier.

"That's enough," he said with groan, stilling her hands. He sucked in a deep breath. "Careful, there, or this will be over before it starts. And I want to take my time and savor you."

Easing her hands away, he raised them to his lips,

kissing one palm, then the other. Rolling to his elbow, he raised her hands above her head, holding her wrists captive. Then he began feathering kisses down the inside of her right arm. At the bend of her elbow, he found a spot that shot shafts of light through her. Moments later he found another sensitive area under her arm.

"You taste so good. Like sunlight and pine."

His mouth found her nipple, and kissed it until it was throbbing.

"Jeff, please . . ."

He raised his head and smiled down at her.

"You'll take me to paradise, my lovely, but not just yet."

Moving up her body, he kissed the pulse point on her left wrist. There were more sensitive places on her left side than on her right, and he found every one. By the time he reached her left breast, she was panting.

"Jeff . . . Jeff . . . please . . . you're killing me."

She moistened her lips, and, watching her, he realized that she didn't know how sexy she looked.

"Ah, Calypso . . . my Calypso . . . you're so beautiful. So shy, but full of passion and fire. So fragile and alone."

"Oh, Jeff . . ." she said, lifting her head toward him, pressing her lips to his.

With a moan he rolled onto her, branding her with his heat as he claimed her lips. His tongue performed magic, and his finger found her again, probing her with the same erotic rhythm.

Her hands were free now, and she moved them down to his hips, pressing him closer, grinding herself against him mindlessly.

"Easy, my Calypso. Easy . . ."

He lifted his weight off her, and, parting her legs, knelt between them. Then, opening her soft petals, he gently pressed inside her.

He saw the pain on her face and waited until she

opened her eyes and looked at him. Her eyes glowed
with knowledge and desire.

"It's okay now."

"You're sure?"

She nodded, smiling at him, and suddenly it *was*
okay. He moved gently, filling her, making her complete, and as she watched, a look of wonder softened
his face.

"So warm. So soft. Like the petals of a flower."

She could feel him moving inside her, seeking her
honey, her nectar, and she opened herself to him.

And finally she knew what it was like to be a woman.

The beauty of the moment caught her by surprise,
and she could only lie there feeling warm and exultant.

Then she began to worry about Jeff. She thought she
had heard him call out as the sun shimmered around
her, but he was lying on her breast, breathing heavily,
and she couldn't see the expression on his face. Had
she pleased him as much as he had pleased her? Had
she made him feel as if he wanted to live and die and
fly all at the same time?

"Thank you," she said tentatively, wanting to say a
lot more but not knowing just what.

He raised his head and smiled down at her, a soft,
sexy smile, which made her melt again. "I should be
thanking you."

"Did I do all right?"

"All right! You were fantastic." Laughing breathlessly
he rolled off her, pulling her so she lay beside him. One
hand caressed her body, stroking her as if she were the
fragile petals of her namesake.

After a while he said softly, "You are an absolutely
amazing woman, my Calypso. One moment you're fighting a forest fire like a trouper, and the next moment
you're making me feel things I've never felt before."

"I'm glad." She snuggled closer, listening to his pounding heart while contentment seeped into her bones.

He touched her hair gently, lifting the damp curls off her temple.

Finally he sighed. "Calypso, my love. We have to get moving."

"Hmm."

"I should've been at Andrews creek at noon."

She raised her head and looked at him. "You mean we have to leave?"

He chuckled. "What happened to the fire fighter who wanted to hike out to base camp in the middle of the night?"

"She'd much prefer to stay here and make love with you." Caly gasped at her newfound boldness. "I'm sorry. I didn't mean that."

Jeff lowered his head. "It's a great idea." He kissed her slowly, thoroughly, whispering against her lips, "The meeting can wait."

Five

"How are you making out?" Jeff called back to Caly as she rounded a steep bend in the trail.

"Fine," she reassured him, and waited until he headed out before kicking Old Darb into a walk.

The fact was, she wasn't fine. She was a real mess. All he had to do was look at her and she melted. If she weren't careful, she'd fall in love with Jeff—and that would be disastrous.

Where was her independence? Where was her backbone? Where was this all going to end?

He probably felt sorry for her and was just being a gentleman, a knight of the range. After all, she had almost begged him to make love to her. But, no matter, she didn't want what they'd shared to end. She loved the way he made her feel. Maybe they could have an affair for the rest of the summer. Jeff had said that he worked on a ranch near Winthrop, so maybe they could see each other when she wasn't out on a fire or he wasn't out with the cattle.

She began whistling, "Oh, What a Beautiful Morning."

Hearing the whistle, Jeff glanced back across Lady,

the pack horse he was leading, noting how easily Caly rode the bay.

She was such a funny mixture, so clumsy in the cabin, but get her outdoors and she was something else. She was riding Old Darb as if she'd been raised in the saddle, and it took a damn good horsewoman to ride the steep mountain trails. She could whistle such a beautiful tune, but she sounded awful if she whistled when she was upset.

He wished he could wave a magic wand and take care of everything for her. He knew she wouldn't stand for it, but it was part of his nature. Babs, his mother's housekeeper, maintained that "Worry" should have been his middle name. Not that he didn't have reason to worry.

It was the hottest, driest summer in history, and the wind was sucking the moisture out of the hay fields faster than the twenty-four-hour irrigation could replace it. The cuttings were so poor, he'd have to buy hay to keep his breeding stock over the winter. And he'd have to buy it soon, before the prices went sky-high. It was either that, or sell off some of his breeding stock, which he didn't want to do. Cattle prices were the lowest in ten years, and he was just building up his herd.

The dry conditions in the forest were playing havoc, too, with the logging operation, which might prove disastrous for Mary Ellen and her husband, Russ. At least there were more tourists at the lodge that summer, and Bonnie Sue and Michael were having a good season. And Nancy Jane and Brian were making a big success of their art gallery in Seattle. His sisters would be fine, but his mother was another matter. The heat wasn't good for her, and she was looking much frailer that summer. He wished her beau, Bill, would stop being such a stubborn old fool and ask her to marry him. They both deserved to be happy.

His heart sank into his boots as he finally admitted to

himself his number-one concern. Caly. He shuddered, thinking about what would happen when they got down off the mountain. Caly would be sent out on another fire, and he'd spend his time worrying about her safety.

And he had reason to worry. He felt sick as he visualized the mass of bruises he'd discovered on her backside when they were dressing. Caly had passed them off, saying that she bruised easily. But doggone, he thought, that wasn't going to happen again if he could help it.

They'd get married the next day, or at least as fast as the law would allow. Then she'd never have to fight another fire.

He wished she were closer, so he could ask her. He should've asked that morning, but they'd been too busy making love. Why hadn't he done it earlier? Maybe the men wouldn't be at the corrals, and he could ask her then.

Both Rob and Ted were there, leaning against the fender of the blue stock truck. The Bell Jet Ranger helicopter sat in the clearing across the road.

"Hey, boss, what took you so long?" Ted called, chewing on a long straw as he watched them approach.

"You had us worried," Rob said, pushing his aviator sunglasses up into his blond hair. "I was about ready to come looking for you."

Spitting out the straw, Ted straightened up and hobbled toward them. "Did ya run into some trouble?"

"No. No trouble," Jeff replied, pulling Buck to a halt beside the old cowboy. Caly reined in behind him.

"What do you mean, no trouble?" Rob asked, glancing back and forth between Jeff and Caly with a speculative look on his handsome face. "We leave you up on that mountain alone, and you come down with a lovely lady."

"And sporting a black eye," Ted added. "Sure looks like trouble to me, boss."

Jeff laughed at their teasing, then glanced back at

Caly. She had dismounted and was hauling the equipment off Lady. Swinging down, he moved to help, and jumped back as the bundle of tools landed at his feet.

Her amber eyes snapped at him, and he could almost feel her hair bristle. Lord, now what had he done?

Frowning in puzzlement, he picked up the bundle and half herded her toward the men who had come forward to catch the reins of the horses.

"Boys, I want you to meet Caly Robbins," he said proudly. "Caly, this is Ted Patterson and Rob Morris."

On another occasion he would've laughed at the expression on Ted's face. Despite her scorched shirt and borrowed jeans, Caly was one beautiful lady.

She smiled at Ted, then batted her long eyelashes at Rob, who was quick to take her hand. The helicopter pilot, with his blue eyes, blond hair, and year-round tan, was good for business. His famous smile kept the female guests happy and anxious to return for another stay at Rendezvous Lodge. Rob turned the full force of his smile on Caly.

Caly smiled back sweetly.

Jeff frowned.

She was flirting with the men, and they were lapping it up! he realized. Ted was old enough to be her father, but Rob was another matter. He was too darned handsome for Jeff to have peace of mind. He'd make damn sure Rob knew that Caly was his.

"I can see why you're late for your meeting, boss. Where did this lovely lady come from?" Rob asked, looking as if he wanted to kiss her hand. Instead he released it. Caly stepped back, her gaze darting between Jeff and Rob.

"Straight from heaven." Jeff meant every word, but realized how corny he sounded. He chuckled, trying to hide his feelings. "At first I thought you boys had forgotten your promise and had sent me another woman for my birthday present."

Ted whinnied, slapping his thigh. "Hey, boss, last year's was a real humdinger, wasn't she?"

Rob laughed, his blue eyes dancing. "I'll never forget the look on your face when that actress crashed your dinner party at the lodge and shoved 'your baby' at you."

"I'll never forget the look on my mother's face, either." Jeff's chuckle died as Caly shot him a killing look. "But I soon found out that I was wrong about Caly, here. She's a Smokejumper. We had a fire up at Moon Ridge," he added hastily, wishing he'd kept his big mouth shut. Caly didn't look as if she appreciated the joke. How could she, he thought, when he'd never explained why he'd kissed her the first time?

"Everything okay? Cattle still there?" Ted asked, pulling at his earlobe.

"Yeah. We got it under control," Jeff said, concerned about Caly's reactions, wondering if she was going to blow. She kicked viciously at a dried cow pat, then looked up at him meaningfully.

"Well, you still might make that meeting if we hurry," Rob said. "Michael was going to try and delay the fella at the lodge."

Jeff let out a deep breath, feeling totally frustrated. All he wanted to do was take Caly off someplace and explain things, but the meeting was important—not only to him, but to a lot of the other folks in the valley.

"Then let's get this show on the road. Fire up the chopper, Rob, while we load this stuff," he said, becoming very businesslike. "We'll drop Caly at the Smokejumpers' base on the way."

He strolled across the gravel road toward the blue-and-white helicopter, and the men followed with the rest of the equipment.

Caly stumbled along in the rear, numb with confusion and anger. She stood by the helicopter, vaguely noting that Rendezvous Lodge was written on its side, while Rob started the preflight checks and Jeff and Ted loaded the equipment. When they were finished, she crawled into a rear seat, trying to ignore Jeff, who climbed in beside her.

"Hope to see you at the ranch soon, miss," Ted said as he closed her door and hobbled off toward the waiting horses.

"You okay?" Jeff asked, touching her shoulder in concern.

She nodded, taking refuge in the noise as Rob started the engine. Jeff touched her again, and she hunched away from him, pressing against the side of the helicopter.

She wasn't okay. Her cowboy wasn't a cowboy. He owned a ranch and a helicopter and a lodge. He was rich, and she knew from bitter experience how the rich used their money to hurt people.

He was no better than her grandfather Valemount. All she meant to Jeff was a one-night stand, a roll in the hay, a joke to be bantered around with the boys. He'd used her.

She closed her eyes, forcing back the burning tears. Dammit, she wasn't going to cry. She never cried, and this no-good, two-bit rancher wasn't going to make her, no matter how much he had hurt her.

Jeff touched her hair, and she jerked her head away, pressing it closer to the window. Trying to block the memories, she concentrated on the scenery. Jagged peaks of the North Cascade Mountains marched along the western horizon. Below them, tree-covered mountain ranges fell away to the sandstone foothills that rimmed the valleys of the Chewack and Methow rivers. Silver-green sage and dark-green bitter bush covered the brown grassland. The only relief in the barren landscape was the cottonwood trees in the river valley and the occasional green of an irrigated hay field or orchard. It was ranching country, but there wasn't a single cow on the range, making Caly realize just how important the mountain grass was to the ranchers.

For a moment she wished that she were back in the mountains again with her Virginian. But Jeff wasn't the Virginian. It had all been a dream—a sweet, beautiful dream with a lousy ending.

The North Cascades Smokejumper base, which was located on a flat bench of land above the Methow River, lay directly below. Thank heaven, she thought; the sooner she got away from Jeff, the better.

After obtaining clearance, Rob landed the helicopter on the tarmac between the brown wooden building that served as the office and the corrugated metal warehouse that held their cache of fire-fighting equipment.

Caly climbed out of the chopper, instinctively ducking to avoid the downdraft of its slapping blades. Turning to pull out her gear, she saw that Jeff was already removing it from his side of the helicopter. Rounding the nose, she stopped him.

"Leave it. I'll manage," she said sharply.

He frowned, shrugged, and then, holding his Stetson on his head, sauntered off to the office. Zeke Olsen, a rangy, balding man, came out to meet Jeff, shook his hand, and slapped him on the back. After giving Caly a quick glance and a satisfied nod, he led Jeff into the office.

Maurice Belchard, small and wiry but tough, trotted out to meet Caly.

"Glad you're back, Cal. Sure missed your smiling face," he said as he lifted a bundle onto his shoulder and took off toward the loft. After waving at Rob, who had remained at the controls of the idling chopper, Caly picked up the rest of the equipment and followed Maurice.

She liked Maurice. He was a schoolteacher in Seattle, and lived for the summers, when he could revel in the excitement of being a Smokejumper. Many of the Smokejumpers were students who were working their way through college, or teachers who could take the summers off. Once they had a taste of Smokejumping they came back year after year. Caly, with her four years of experience, felt like a relative newcomer. But they all—or almost all—had one thing in common. They loved the excitement, camaraderie, and action of being a Smokejumper.

Entering the paraloft, Caly glanced at the Jump List board, the center of operations. With a sinking feeling, she noted that her name was second from the top, under Brad's. Dammit. He'd be boss on the next fire.

Moving into the room, she dropped her parachute on one of the three repacking tables. Once packed, the parachutes were stored on shelves along one wall. Quick-suit-up racks stood along another wall. Only five suits hung on the racks, which meant that the rest of the crew was out on a fire. Twenty-four Smokejumpers were assigned to the base, and even during a normal season they kept busy. This year had been horrendous.

"Where's everyone?" she asked Maurice, who had started unpacking her equipment.

Brad Parks entered the loft. With his blond hair and muscular physique he could have passed as a Greek god, except for his receding chin. Never trust a man with a weak chin, her grandfather had warned her. And he was right, Brad was a spoiled brat. "Looking for me, sweetie?" Brad asked.

"Not particularly." Caly watched him steadily as his blue eyes raked her up and down, taking in her tattered shirt and borrowed jeans.

"Two of the guys are out on a spot fire, and we sent a relief crew over to Redmond last night." Maurice answered her question quickly. He didn't like Brad, either, and he made no bones about it.

Brad ignored him, leering at Caly. "Lover boy says you had to fight a fire, after all, and he seems pretty upset about something. I'll wager it's that black eye he's sporting. What happened? Did he get too close?"

He'd been making similar remarks all summer, and it was getting to her. What really burned her was that

Brad was spoiling her relationship with the other men. In the past, she had always had fun with the men on the fire crews, taking part in the pranks and laughing when one was played on her. Now she was constantly on guard against the possibility that they would believe the lies Brad was spreading about her.

She had learned quickly that her only defense was to keep her cool. That tactic usually smothered Brad's comments faster than anything. But it was hard keeping her cool when she couldn't help but wonder if something was different about her. Could the men tell that she had made love with Jeff?

"There sure'n hell was a fire, and since you weren't there he had to help fight it," she said pointedly, trying to use Brad's guilt to sidetrack him.

"Likely story," Brad said with a sneer. "Probably got beat up fighting off your hot bod."

She should've known that Brad wouldn't feel guilty about letting her jump alone.

Afraid that she'd blow up, Caly stalked outside. She'd had enough of Brad Parks. Hot air rose off the tarmac and blasted her, then shimmered away across the sage-filled range. She'd thought it was hot in the mountains, but it was at least a hundred in the camp.

Maurice and Brad joined her just as Zeke and Jeff walked out of the office and down the steps.

Zeke smiled in approval as he looked at Caly. "Take the rest of the day off, Red." Turning to Brad, he said, "Parks, I want to see you in the office. Now."

All the Smokejumpers thought the world of Zeke. He was a stern jump master, who, at the beginning of each season, made them train until they could land on a dime. His jumpers knew they were the best in the business, and they revered as well as respected Zeke.

And they did their damnedest to make sure he never spoke to them in the tone of voice he'd used to address Brad.

Caly wondered briefly why Zeke was ready to chew

Brad out. Surely Jeff hadn't told him what had happened on the jump. Damn him, anyway. He shouldn't have been interfering in her business.

She glared daggers at Jeff as he approached. He held out his hand, and she was forced to take it because of the other men.

"Thanks for everything," he said softly, his hand transmitting more than thanks. "I'll drop by tonight."

"Don't bother," she choked out, snatching her hand away. She couldn't bear to touch him, couldn't bear to stand next to the man who had hurt her but still had the power to move her with the mere touch of his hand. Swinging around, she took off at a trot across the tarmac, toward the parking lot and her Kawasaki 175.

Some of the men stayed in the corrugated-tin-roofed bunkhouses on base, but Caly had decided to board in Winthrop that year. A coincidence had brought her to the home of Zeke Olsen and his wife, Myra. Arriving in town, she'd asked the friendly-faced Myra, who worked in the post office, about local accommodations, and had accepted her offer of room and board. It wasn't until Zeke came home that night that she realized she would be living with her boss. He had offered no objection, and Caly had learned that it was normal for one of the Smokejumpers to board with them for the summer. Myra contended that it kept them young to have young people around. Their two children were grown and unfortunately couldn't come home very often.

The Smokejumpers' base was four miles from Winthrop, and within minutes Caly had parked her bike in front of the white picket fence that surrounded the flower-filled yard and white two-story house.

Myra met her in the hall. She was a small lady with large hips and bosom to match. Her bright brown eyes peered through thick lenses, missing nothing.

"You look beat, dearie," she said, her round face

wrinkled in concern. "You go right up and have your shower, and I'll fix you something to eat."

Caly had just finished supper and was sitting at the kitchen table drinking a third cup of Myra's delicious coffee, when a knock sounded on the front door. Myra went to answer it, returning moments later with Jeff, who must have come straight from the meeting. He was wearing the same clothes he'd had on earlier and looked exhausted. Caly glanced away, unable to face his black eye or, worse yet, the green one that was looking at her with such emotion.

Jeff examined her, taking in her slumping shoulders and lackluster expression. He wanted to gather her into his arms and hold her and kiss her, and then take her back to the ranch and coddle her and make love to her.

Myra's eyes darted back and forth between them.

"Sit down, Jeff, and have some coffee," she told him, pouring some into a brown mug and setting it on the table.

Jeff sank obediently into the chair next to Caly's and grabbed the coffee cup in both hands, needing something to hold on to so he wouldn't reach out and touch her.

"I came as soon as I could."

"I told you not to bother." She tapped her mug on the table, then covered it with her hand, shaking her head at Myra, who was holding the coffeepot over it.

Jeff cleared his throat, then took a sip of coffee. "But I want to explain—"

"There's no need."

"Give me a break, Caly." He set the mug down with a restrained thud.

"I'll leave you two alone. You seem to have a lot to talk about," Myra said knowingly as she left the kitchen, closing the door behind her.

Caly barely waited until Myra was out of the room

before bursting into speech. "You couldn't wait to have a good laugh with the boys, could you?"

A flush started in the curly hair at the base of his throat and rose up to his face. He reached out a hand to her. She slapped it away, then sat on her hands.

"Caly, I didn't mean—"

"That's all I was to you, a little fling in the mountains." She wiggled on her hands. "You thought the boys had sent me in to help you celebrate your birthday, but when you found out the truth, it didn't matter one damn bit. You used me."

He jerked as if he'd been shot, knocking over the mug. Coffee spilled across the red plastic tablecloth.

A muscle on the side of his mouth twitched. "You . . ." His voice cracked, and he swallowed hard before he tried to speak again. "You . . . think that I . . . was using you?"

"Yes." She almost yelled the word.

"What kind of man do you think I am?" He thumped the table with his clenched fist, then forced his palm open. Coffee soaked into the cuff of his blue shirt. "Sure, the boys have been sending me a woman every year for my birthday . . . but they know, and the women know, that nothing ever happens." He raked his hand through his hair. "Lord, Caly, I'm not some hot-shot stud. I haven't been with a woman since Christmas. . . ." His voice trailed off, and he sat there shaking his head, looking hurt.

It was impossible not to believe him, but that didn't let him off the hook. "Okay, so maybe you weren't out to make a score. But I've given you loads of stories to keep you and the boys laughing all winter." She wiggled again, wanting desperately to get up and pace. "I can just hear it now. 'Oh, by the way, did I tell you about the time she dropped the frying pan on my toe?' "

"You've got it all wrong." He touched his eye, then wiped his hand wearily across his face. "I love you, Caly. I want to marry you."

"Marry me!" Her hands flew to her mouth. "You're crazy. You've only known me forty-eight hours. You can't be serious."

"I'm dead serious. I've loved you for at least forty-seven of those forty-eight hours."

"Then you *are* crazy. You don't know what you're doing."

"I'm thirty-five years old. I should know what I'm doing by now."

She folded her hands carefully in front of her, striving to be calm. "That's it. You've just turned thirty-five and you think that it's time to marry and settle down, so you asked the first woman who came along."

He sat absolutely still, the color draining from his face. His tone of voice was glacial.

"Calypso Robbins, you are making me very angry."

"I'm not the right woman for you," she said earnestly.

"But—"

"I can't cook or sew or do any of those womanly things."

He snorted. "You could've fooled me. That was a woman who made love to me this morning. I'd bet the ranch that you could learn to cook and sew if you put your mind to it."

She bowed her head. "You see. You want to change me."

Jeff slipped to his knees on the floor beside her chair. "I love you, Caly. Please marry me."

She raised her eyes in surprise. Now what was he doing? He shouldn't have been getting down on his knees. She turned away, not wanting to see the pain and hope that were written all over his face.

She swallowed hard. "No," she said huskily.

He didn't touch her, and his voice was so low that she could barely hear it.

"Will you at least tell me that you forgive me? I didn't mean to hurt you."

"Just go away and leave me alone," she whispered, burying her head in her hands.

She felt him rise to his feet. His hands trembled as he touched her hair. She shrank away.

"I'll say good-bye, then, my Calypso."

He went out the back door, closing it softly. Caly remained in her chair, too exhausted to move, too exhausted to think, too exhausted to cry. She was still there when Myra bustled into the kitchen.

"What happened, dearie? Jeff drove off without saying good-bye." She spotted the coffee immediately and started mopping it up.

Caly could only shake her head.

"Has he done something to hurt you?" Myra fixed her bright eyes on Caly.

Caly shook her head again.

"Then why did he roar out of here in his big Mercedes as if he were trying to outrun a prairie fire?"

Raising her head, Caly looked at the concerned woman and blurted out, "Because I told him to leave."

"Now, you just tell me what is going on. If that young scalawag has done anything to hurt you, Zeke will make sure that he does right by you."

It took a second for her meaning to sink in, and when it did, Caly managed a weak smile.

"That won't be necessary. Jeff asked me to marry him."

"He did? Then what's all the fuss about?"

"I refused."

For once Myra was almost at a loss for words. "Why?"

"Because I don't want to."

Myra looked at her in amazement. "But I don't understand. Jeff's the catch of the valley. In fact, Zeke and I were thinking of introducing you to him. We'd almost given up hope that he'd ever fall in love again, and now that he has, it's a crying shame that you won't marry him." Whipping off her glasses, she polished them with the corner of her apron. Putting them on again, she peered sternly at Caly. "Are you sure you won't marry him, dearie?"

Caly shook her head.

"You're hurting a fine man, young lady. A fine man."

"I know," Caly whispered. "But it just wouldn't work." Jumping to her feet, she ran out of the room.

Caly spent a sleepless night staring blindly at the faded Calypso orchids she'd brought with her and thinking about the cowboy who had given them to her.

Jeff had said that he loved her and wanted to marry her, but she knew it wouldn't work. He'd want to change her, just as the Valemounts had tried to do. Her mother's rich parents hadn't liked one thing about the seven-year-old ragamuffin who'd turned up unexpectedly at their mansion door, and had promptly set out to correct the situation. Wanting their love and approval, she'd tried desperately to please them, but soon realized that in their eyes she could do nothing right. The summer had been a nightmare. Luckily Big Red had come to see her after the fire season was over and had rescued her. It had taken him a year to teach her to whistle again. She'd been afraid to trust, afraid to love anyone else—until Jeff. Until he'd brought her the orchids.

She brushed the petals against her lips.

She cradled the flowers in the palm of her hand, knowing that despite what had happened, she still trusted him. But loving him would be a disaster. She definitely was not the right woman for him, and she wasn't about to change.

Raising the dead flowers to her lips, she kissed them, then placed them carefully between the pages of a battered hardback book and slid it under her pillow.

Calypso orchids could not be transplanted.

• • •

Myra was not her usual talkative self the next morning, and Caly felt uneasy in the abnormal silence. At least Zeke treated her the same, so Myra must not have said anything to him, or if she had, he'd decided that it was none of his business.

Most of the twenty-four Smokejumpers had returned to base, and after their calisthenics and morning run around the field, they spent the rest of the day repairing and repacking equipment. Caly, who kept her motorbike tuned to perfection, was assigned to service the chain saws. Although the men teased her about her hot-rod tendencies, they came by between jobs to ask her how they could get better performances out of their bikes, cars, or pickups. Brad also stopped by frequently, breaking in on their discussions with sly innuendos and generally making himself obnoxious.

Consequently, when the men invited her to go to the saloon in Twisp with them, she refused. She couldn't have borne another minute in Brad's company, and she was still uncertain about whether the other men were giving credence to what he was saying about her. It made her mad, though, because she enjoyed going for a beer with the guys.

Myra made no comment because Zeke, who had accompanied the crew, hadn't returned for supper. She and Caly were sitting in the living room when he came home later that evening. Myra was crocheting and Caly was reading *The Virginian* for the fifty-third time. She didn't know why she was reading it—it made her feel sad, but it was also soothing medicine for her soul.

Zeke settled his long body into the big leather chair, the only piece of furniture not covered with doilies. Caly had coveted that chair all summer, feeling uncomfortable on the overstuffed, over-doilied sofa. Even Myra's favorite spot, the rocking chair, would have been more comfortable.

Zeke hemmed and hawed while he lit his pipe. Caly glanced up and caught him looking at her over his cupped hand. "What's with you and Brad Parks?" he asked once his pipe was lit to his satisfaction.

Caly smiled at Zeke uneasily, laying the dog-eared book aside. "Nothing."

Zeke didn't seem to be condemning her, so Caly decided that it was time to level with him. Myra was watching her with a disappointed look in her eyes, which made Caly want to explain. How could Myra think that she would turn down marriage to Jeff and be interested in a toad like Brad?

"We had a run-in when we were in training camp," she continued. "He was coming on pretty strong, and I'm afraid I floored him with a punch."

Zeke puffed away. "Hmm. That explains it, then," he muttered around the stem of the pipe.

"I know he's been spreading rumors about me this year, but I can't do much about it. That's why I don't go out with the boys."

"Well, you won't have to worry about Parks any longer." Zeke took his pipe out of his mouth. "Not after what Jeff did to him tonight."

Caly jerked upright. "Jeff? What's Jeff got to do with this?" Leaning over, she rescued the doily that had somehow fallen off the arm of the sofa.

Zeke took his time, puffing on his pipe and blowing a cloud of smoke out of the corner of his mouth. Finally he removed his pipe and gave her a broad grin.

"Well, he was in the saloon when we arrived, and Parks made a remark about his black eye. Jeff let it pass without comment, and I thought that was the end of things." He paused and puffed again, looking tickled. Caly sat forward, then reached around to pull another doily up behind her, wishing he'd get on with his story.

Myra stopped crocheting and leveled her bright eyes on Zeke.

"And then what happened?" Myra asked the question that Caly was itching to ask.

"Then Parks started making snide remarks about Red to the other men."

"And?" Myra prompted.

"And Jeff grabbed him by the scruff of his neck and made him admit that he was a no-good, lying scoundrel."

"Jeff did that!" Caly said, her voice squeaking. He'd fought for her honor even though she'd refused to marry him.

"Yep. Unfortunately, Parks admitted it right away, so Jeff didn't get a chance to mark him up any." He puffed again.

"Surely that's not the end of the story, Zeke Olsen. Out with it," Myra said, her tone insistent.

"After he threw Parks outside, Jeff turned around and challenged the rest of us." He puffed. "There was one of him and more than a dozen of us."

He peered over his pipe at Caly, and she closed her eyes in dismay. Jeff had gotten into a saloon brawl and had been beaten up, and it was all her fault.

Six

"Zeke, you old goat, stop teasing the poor girl."

Caly opened her eyes to find Zeke grinning at her.

"The men were quick to tell him that they took no stock in what Parks has been saying about you, Red, nor do they hold with the way he's been treating you. That seemed to sit well with Jeff, and he bought us all a drink and left."

He focused his attention on his pipe again. Myra nodded in approval and went back to her crocheting. Caly sat on the edge of the couch, tense with indecision.

Zeke finally got his pipe going to his satisfaction. "The men do respect you, by the way, despite what Parks has been saying. I knew how they felt, or I'd have stopped him a long time ago. I also figured you could handle yourself if it came to a blowup, so I stayed out of it, as I would if you were a man."

"Thank you." She was pleased beyond words that Zeke respected her and her independence. His assurances that her fellow Smokejumpers thought she was okay would make the rest of the summer bearable.

"Anyway, you won't have to worry about Parks. I'm transferring him out tomorrow."

"You don't have to do that."

"The two of you shouldn't be in the same camp, and I'd rather keep you, Red." He cleared his throat. "You're a much better man."

High praise, indeed, from Zeke, she realized. "Thank you," she said again, embarrassed by the rush of good feeling that flowed through her.

"I'm not the man you should be thanking," Zeke suggested slyly, tapping his pipe into the palm of his hand.

Zeke was right. It was Jeff who had defended her honor. It was Jeff who had risked injury to himself and his reputation because of her. The Virginian had done the same thing for the schoolmarm he'd just met, and Caly always had thought it was the most romantic thing she'd ever read. But Jeff had done even better. He had defended her despite the fact that she had turned down his proposal of marriage. He *was* a knight of the range.

She jumped to her feet. "You're right. I must go and thank Jeff. Where does he live?"

"Do you think it's wise to see him at this time of night, dearie?" Myra asked, looking up from her flying hook.

Caly smiled at her from the door. "Probably not, but then, I've never been known for being wise. Anyway, if I wait until tomorrow, I might be shipped out on a fire, and heaven knows when I'll see him again—and by then it'll be too late."

"She's right, Myra. Besides, from the way Jeff looked tonight, I think he'd appreciate her visit. His mother and Babs are home, so you don't have to worry about her reputation."

"Don't you think you should at least change your clothes?" Myra asked.

Caly glanced down at her kelly-green shirt and faded blue jeans. Rainbow iron-on patches held the right knee of her jeans together; otherwise they were in pretty good shape.

"I don't have time. Besides, Jeff has seen me looking a lot worse than this."

Following Zeke's directions, Caly followed the Methow River Valley for a few miles, then turned into a long lane lined with elegant Lombardy poplars. The poplars also ringed a sprawling, two-story log house, separating it from the barns and corrals that stretched across the river flat. Parking her bike in front of the double garage, she dashed through the sprinklers to the screened veranda that skirted the front and side of the house. Hurriedly, before she changed her mind, she rapped loudly on the screen door.

The outside light flicked on beside her. The main door opened, and Jeff walked across the veranda.

"Caly! What are you doing here?" Opening the screen door, he stared down at her in disbelief.

She stared back, speechless. His blue shirt hung open, and all she wanted to do was touch the springy curls that covered his chest, to lay her head against the warm skin. Heat flooded through her as she remembered how his naked body had felt against hers. So sensuous, seductive, exciting. Raising her gaze, she saw the hopeful look on his face.

"Caly?"

"I . . . could I talk to you for a minute?" How could she remain cool and calm when her heart started pounding like a woodpecker on a hollow tree at the sight of him? Now that she was there, she wished she'd just phoned to thank him.

"Come in." He moved back, pulling the door with him, carefully avoiding his bare toes.

Caly followed, tripping on the top step and sprawling forward. With a startled grunt, Jeff caught her, holding her close against his hard, muscular frame. She heard his heart thudding and his ragged breathing before he slowly released her. Caly clung to him a moment, wanting his kiss, then pulled back. What was the matter with her? she thought angrily. Just because they had made love once didn't mean that they would again. And to make matters worse, Jeff was acting as if nothing had happened between them.

"Sorry. I should've warned you about the step. It's higher than the rest," he said in apology, waving her toward a group of chairs and a wooden swing that hung from a beam on two thick ropes. "Let's sit out here. I'd ask you in, but mother and Babs, our housekeeper, are just getting ready for bed." So much for her chaperones.

Shaken by her lack of control, Caly collapsed gratefully on the first thing she saw—the swing, which promptly threw her on the floor.

The swing started its downward arc, and Jeff caught it just before it clunked her on the head. He snorted, then coughed, and Caly knew he was trying hard to stifle a laugh. She didn't blame him. Her clumsiness had gone past the point of being ridiculous. It was absurd!

"Go ahead. Laugh," she said in resignation. "You should know by now that I'm a walking disaster whenever I'm around you."

"You do seem to have a problem, Li'l Red," Jeff said as he helped her to her feet. He guided her into the swing and sat down beside her. The swing creaked, then swayed. Caly took a deep breath. Somehow the fact that he held her hand made her feel good about being there, even though she was making a fool of herself.

"Zeke told me what happened in the saloon," she said. "I wanted to thank you for standing up for me."

"Forget it, Caly. It was nothing," he said, squeezing her hand.

"Nothing, my big foot. It could've turned into a real

ugly scene and you could have been hurt and you might have been arrested and what would people have thought of you and what would your mother say and—"

"Hey, it's okay." Laughing softly, he ran a finger across her cheek. She rested her head against the palm of his hand, remembering what it had been like to lie next to this man, to make love to him. Had it only been the day before? It seemed like months.

She sighed.

"What's wrong, Li'l Red?"

Everything. Nothing. Why was she so confused? Sighing again, she made an effort to collect her scattered thoughts. "What I can't figure out is why you did it."

He captured her face between his palms, turning it so he could stare into her eyes. "Simple," he said in a husky whisper. "I couldn't stand there and let him run down the character of the woman I love."

Overcome by an irresistible urge, Caly leaned forward and kissed him on his lips. He felt so good. He tasted so good. He smelled good, too, the way a man should.

Dammit, what was she doing kissing him? She drew back. Jeff smiled at her, looking like a little boy who had just received his first pony.

He gave the swing a big push, then spent the next few seconds bringing it back under control. Finally he steadied the swing—and his emotions—down enough to pull her into his arms. She rolled her head into the hollow of his shoulder and relaxed.

"This Brad Parks. What's he to you?" Jeff asked after they had swung awhile in companionable silence.

"The only other man who's kissed me," she blurted out without thinking.

"Oh." His body went very still, and the swing stopped.

"And I knocked him flat." She smiled up at him impishly. "But I couldn't do that to you, could I?" Caly gently traced a circle around his blackened eye.

"I wouldn't be too sure about that." He kissed the inside of her wrist.

Disconcerted, Caly went on. "After the way I treated you last night, I thought you'd have nothing more to do with me, much less that you'd defend me in a saloon brawl."

"What did you expect me to do? Laugh it off?" Wearily he passed his free hand over his eyes. "I love you, my Calypso. Despite the impression I might've given you, I'd . . . cut off my arm before I'd intentionally do or say anything to hurt you or hurt your reputation."

She wiggled her head into a more comfortable position against his shoulder. "You're an honorable man."

"I'd like to think so. But more importantly, I want you to believe it."

She sighed. "I do, Jeff. I guess I was overreacting yesterday. I didn't know what to think—about you, about myself, about what we'd done. And then the men looked at me, and you laughed and . . ."

He began running his fingers through her hair, lifting the curls gently. "They were looking at a beautiful woman and envying me. I laughed because I was hoping they wouldn't guess that you'd lassoed my heart." He rolled a curl between his fingers, loving the way its softness felt against his rough skin. "Not that it matters much now. The whole valley will know, after what happened tonight."

"Oh, Jeff." She buried her face against his warm chest, thinking about how much embarrassment she had caused him.

"Marry me, my Calypso," he said, resting his cheek against her hair. "Make an honest man out of me."

"I can't." Her voice was muffled.

"Why?" He nuzzled her hair with his lips, kissing her once, then again.

The warmth of his body seeped into her, and the gentle persuasion of his kisses made it difficult for

Caly to think. "Because it's too soon. It's hard to believe that you could fall in love with me so fast."

Jeff's arms tightened around her. "Believe it. You smiled at me and I was a goner."

"It can't be love. It must be infatuation."

"I don't know how you define love. But if love is wanting to cherish you and protect you for the rest of your life, then believe me. I love you." His words filled her, warming her, flooding her with happiness. She snuggled against him, listening to the strong, steady beat of his heart, feeling totally content. After a few moments he continued. "While we were fighting that fire yesterday, all I could think about was that I was going to marry you and you could quit your job."

"You'd want me to quit?" She raised her head and stared at him in dismay.

"Damn right. I couldn't live with watching you go off on a fire and wondering if you'd return alive."

Breaking free of his arms, she got to her feet and headed for the screen door. He followed, catching her by the shoulder and turning her around. "What's the matter, Caly?"

She stared up at him, her eyes bright. "If that's the way you feel, there's no use going any further. You know how important fire fighting is to me. It's my life, and I won't give it up."

"But it won't be your life when you're married to me. You'll be my wife, and that will be your life. You'll be the mother of our children. You can't be a fire fighter."

She felt the hair on the nape of her neck begin to bristle, a sure sign that her temper was reaching gale-force proportions and rising.

"What's the matter with being a fire fighter? Aren't I good enough for you? Are you going to try and make me over too?" She pulled at his arm to loosen his hold.

Jeff stepped back, shaking his head in bewilderment. "I'm not trying to change you. It's normal for a woman to want a husband and children."

"Not this woman." She stood, hands on hips, tapping her foot in irritation.

"Don't you dream about having a husband and children?"

"Nope."

"For heaven's sake, why not?"

She swung away from him, striding down the length of the veranda, then back to confront him. "You tell me why so many people get divorced."

He raked his hand through his hair, bewildered by her question. "I don't know."

"Come on, you must have some thoughts on the matter."

He chewed his lip, considering his answer. "I guess because they're looking for something elusive, and when they find that their mate doesn't have it, they start looking again," he said thoughtfully. "Instead of realizing that what they're really looking for is themselves."

"Which means that a woman must be happy with herself, with who she is, before she can be happy in a marriage."

He didn't like the way this conversation was going. "I guess so," he admitted in frustration.

"Which proves my point. I'm not ready for marriage yet. I have to find out who I am before I'd even consider it."

He sighed, then reached out to touch her face with a hand that trembled. "Will you let me help you?"

She took his hand in both of hers. "I'm afraid to, Jeff." She kissed the back of his hand, then pulled it against her breasts. "You'll try to change me, and instead of finding out who I am, I'll wind up trying to be what you want me to be."

"I won't try to change you, Caly, just help you." His free hand caressed her shoulder.

She stared into his eyes, wishing that she could believe him, but it was so hard. She sighed. "It's something I have to do by myself."

"Okay, but I'll warn you right now, I'm going to do everything in my power to hurry the process along," he said huskily.

His hand moved to the back of her head, supporting it as his lips captured hers. Sparks of awareness tingled through her, tantalizing her. He shuddered against her, deepening the kiss. Caly gasped as his tongue seared her lips. He moaned softly.

Releasing his hand, she pressed her body against his. She rubbed her breasts back and forth across his bare chest, feeling his heat through the thin cotton of her shirt. Her nipples throbbed, and a flash of fire consumed her as if she were dry kindling. She trembled in his arms, remembering how she'd felt when he'd made love to her—so alive, so aware of every part of her body, and of his.

She wanted him, wanted to feel him inside her, wanted him to take her again to blazing heights.

She wasn't surprised that she'd ignited so quickly. By the feel of his manhood against her, she knew Jeff was just as aroused. They were like two pieces of tinder. When they rubbed themselves together, they flamed into passion.

They had to find a way to be together. She couldn't marry him, not yet, but she desperately needed to be with him. He had awakened a part of her that she'd never known. But it did exist, and she wanted—no, needed—to learn more about it.

Caly broke the kiss enough to gasp against his lips, "Can we just make love?"

Jeff pulled back his head and looked at her in astonishment. "You want an affair?"

"Yes," she whispered, nuzzling the hollow at his throat.

"But why?"

"Because I like the way you make me feel when we're making love." She traced his lips shyly with her forefinger.

With a groan he bent over and claimed her lips again. "And I like the way you make me feel."

Caught up in the ecstasy of his kisses, Caly was certain that he would agree to an affair. Then, with a sigh, he released her lips, and his words blew her hopes away. "I can't have an affair with you."

"Why? Don't you want to make love with me?" she asked, hurt.

"Of course I want to make love with you." He stroked her curls with gentle fingers. "I want to make love with you every time I touch you. Even watching you walk makes me ache for you."

"Then why can't we make love?" Caly raised her head and looked at him.

He cradled her face between the palms of his hand and smiled at her tenderly. "Because everyone in this valley knows what everyone else is doing, and I don't want people talking about you."

She shook her head, brushing his hands aside. "What you really mean is that you don't want people talking about you. After all, you're a big man in the valley, and you have a reputation to protect," she said bitterly, knowing that she was overreacting, but unable to stop the words.

His eyes darkened with pain.

"You've got it all wrong, Caly," he said hoarsely. "I don't give a damn what people say about me, but I do care what they say about the woman I love. I want to marry you, not have an affair with you." A muscle twitched on the side of his mouth. "I want a wife and a mother for my children. Not a summer fling."

Her anger disappeared as she listened to his words. She knew that he spoke the truth, but it didn't make things any easier. She sighed. "Then I guess there's no use in our seeing each other."

"Why?"

"Because I can't marry you if it means I have to give up fire fighting." The look on his face tore a hole in her heart. "I'm sorry, Jeff," she whispered, touching his lips with the tip of one finger.

His hands captured her face again, and his green eye branded her with love. "As I said, I don't give up easily. I've waited too long to find you, my Calypso, and I'm not about to lose you." He possessed her lips in a hard, demanding kiss.

Overwhelmed by the intensity of his feelings, Caly broke away. "I have to go," she said with a gasp.

He pulled her back against him. "In a bit," he said, lowering his head for another kiss. She felt so good in his arms, and he desperately wanted to keep her there. His hands moved up under her loose shirt, finding their way unerringly to the sensitive sides of her breasts. He could feel her thighs trembling against his, and he remembered the way they felt when they were cinched around him. He rocked against her, wanting to be inside her again so badly that he thought he'd burst. She'd been so receptive. So hot. So fulfilling. He wanted her, wanted her, wanted her.

"Oh, Jeff, yes."

Her moan of desire cooled the flames that threatened to destroy his resolve. In another few moments he'd have seduced her right there on the porch, with his mother and Babs just inside the house. He held her off, standing with his forehead touching hers as he fought for control.

"I should have my head examined. How did I ever imagine I could kiss you and not want to make love with you? Come on, my Calypso, I'll walk you to your bike while I still can."

Hand in hand they sprinted across the lawn. Once clear of the sprinklers, he stopped abruptly and turned to look down at her.

"I just thought of something. You might be pregnant."

"What?" she asked in confusion.

"You know that I didn't take any precautions when we made love. I realized at the time that we were running a risk, but I didn't think it would matter, because I hoped you'd marry me right away."

She gave an embarrassed laugh. "But, Jeff, I really—"

"You'll let me know if you are?" His voice brooked no argument, and she realized that he was dead serious.

"I . . . okay. I'll tell you," she agreed, also very serious—and a little frightened. When they were making love, the thought that she might get pregnant had never entered her mind. She'd been too caught up in the pleasure Jeff had shown her.

Suddenly she needed to put some space between them. Releasing his hand, she turned and walked quickly to her bike.

He followed.

"I don't like the idea of your riding around on that bike. You could get killed."

"Jeff," Caly said gently but with a hint of iron in her voice. He heard it, and changed his mind about chiding her further.

"I'm sorry. When you get to know me better, you'll learn that I worry too much. It's a bad habit."

"You only have one?"

"No, but I'll tell you the others another time. I don't want to frighten you off completely."

She smiled up at him as she kicked the bike off the stand. "I don't frighten easily. Remember?"

"Thank heaven for that. I think." He kissed her on the tip of her nose, then stepped back as she swung a leg over the saddle. One look at his bare feet told Caly why he was keeping his distance. At least she hadn't stepped on them while they'd been kissing. My gosh, she thought, his feet were small for such a tall man. She'd have bet hers were almost as big. Big Red had always said that it was lucky that so much of her was turned under. Otherwise she'd have been a giant.

"Are you busy on Sunday?" His words cut into her silly thoughts, and she looked up from his feet to find him watching her with a smile on his face.

"I had planned to stay on base if I wasn't out on a fire. Why?"

"We're having our annual family picnic, and I'd like you to come. It will give you a chance to meet everyone."

She didn't want to meet "everyone" just yet—not when she was feeling so unsure of herself and of Jeff. She needed more time.

"It sure would be nice to have you here," Jeff said wistfully.

The sound of his voice was her undoing.

"I'll come if I can."

"Great. I know they'll love you."

She knew differently. His family wasn't going to love her. They wouldn't even like her. And they definitely wouldn't think that she was good enough for Jeff. She just knew it.

Fighting down her feeling of panic, she muttered, "What can I bring?"

"Just yourself, my love." His voice caressed her like a balm, but her memories were still raw as she roared home on her bike. Memories of another family that should have loved her but didn't. Memories of how much she'd been hurt by the way the Valemounts had treated her. Memories of how they had almost destroyed her.

She wasn't being fair to Jeff's family, she realized. Maybe they'd be different. Maybe they would accept her the way she was.

Yes, she'd go to the picnic. What could she lose? Just her self-confidence and her laughter and her ability to whistle, she thought despairingly.

Caly felt like a basket case when she arrived at the Half Moon Ranch at two on Sunday afternoon . . . on her bike . . . carrying her cake. There'd been many times during the last three days when she had doubted that she'd make the picnic. In fact, if she hadn't insisted that the Smokejumpers be bused home the previous night after they'd finished mopping up the fire on the Colville reserve, she'd still have been sitting in Omak.

Now that she was there, she wished she were back at the fire. At least she knew her way around a fire. A family picnic was something else. She'd never fit in. She just knew that the family wouldn't like her! She had to think positively, she decided.

A red Jaguar sat in the driveway next to a brown Mercedes and a moss-green Volvo. Her Kawasaki 175 definitely did not belong. After hanging her helmet on the seat, she carefully unstrapped the Tupperware cake holder from a carrier on the front of the bike. The carrier had been a cinch to make, compared to the cake.

Thank goodness for Myra, she thought. When she'd learned that Caly had been invited to the family picnic and wanted to take a cake, she'd pitched right in. She even had talked Caly through the project step by step.

Determinedly Caly walked toward the house, noting absently that the trees and lush green lawn made it cool and inviting. It was a welcome relief from the heat and dirt of the last few days.

A tall elderly lady with a leathery tan that spoke of years of being outdoors answered her knock. She had laughing brown eyes and looked so pleasant that Caly hoped she was Jeff's mother.

"Come in, my dear. You must be Caly. I'm Barbara McKay, but everyone calls me Babs. I'm the cook and housekeeper and jack-of-all-trades, y'know. Let me take that." Caly sighed with relief. She had been confident that she could carry it to the door without dropping it, despite her unorthodox method of transportation, but she knew how accident-prone she was around Jeff.

Babs continued. "We'll leave this in the kitchen and then join the family in the back yard."

Caly followed her through the living room, too busy concentrating on her feet to take much note of the furnishings. She had a vague impression of a stone fireplace flanked by ceiling-high bookcases and brown leather furniture.

Babs was still talking as they entered the kitchen, a large room full of sunshine and hanging plants. "I'm so glad you're here. Jeff will be very pleased, y'know. He's been twitchier than a rattler, worrying whether you'd make it. It's about time he had someone of his own at these family get-togethers. Oh, he never complains, and he enjoys himself, but it really isn't the same, y'know."

She set the cake down on the long oak table, which was laden with food. "You didn't need to bring anything, y'know. But thank you anyway. Let's see what it is." Removing the cover, she revealed the creation of chocolate, whipped cream, and cherries.

"It's a black forest cake," Caly said, looking at the cake critically. Myra had advised her to start with something easier, but she'd had her heart set on making this cake.

"It . . . looks fabulous."

Caly missed the housekeeper's slight hesitation. The kirsch smelled pretty strong. Maybe she had been a little lavish with it, but she'd wanted the cake to be sinfully rich.

"I think I should warn—" Babs was cut off by Jeff.

"Caly, honey, I'm glad you're here," he called happily from the back door. Crossing the kitchen, he hugged Caly quickly, then stepped back to devour her with his eyes.

"Are you all right?" he asked in concern, observing the dark smudges under her eyes and the way her shoulders drooped.

"I'm fine." Now that she was in his arms, she was fine. And she felt even better because the eye she'd slugged was no longer black.

He gave her another quick hug. "Thank the good

Lord. Come on, the rest of the family is anxious to meet you. Ah, here's Mother."

A tiny woman with hair the color of fireweed honey appeared at the door, and Jeff stepped away from Caly. Looking at his mother, Caly felt a moment of panic. Dressed in a powder-blue summer dress, Mrs. Adams wasn't like the other ranch women she'd seen in town. They were tanned and robust. Mrs. Adams was pale and fragile and had a helpless air about her, which, Caly realized, would make every man she met want to protect and cherish her. That was just the way Jeff had said he felt about her, too, she remembered with a rush of warmth.

As Jeff made the introductions, Patricia Adams looked Caly over thoroughly, giving her the distinct impression that Jeff's mother found her lacking in every department. Feeling suddenly deflated, Caly concentrated on making sure that she didn't crush the slim hand that Patricia offered. It was surprisingly strong, and Caly was sure hers felt like a dead fish.

"I'm p-pleased to m-meet you," she stammered, wiping her damp palm on her pant leg. Now she was sounding like an imbecile, to boot.

Mrs. Adams took Jeff's arm, clinging to it. "Let's go and meet the others," she said coolly, guiding Jeff out the door, leaving Caly and Babs to follow.

The manicured back yard overflowed with people. Jeff introduced her to everyone, but it was too confusing to remember their names and who belonged to whom, and she was thankful when he settled her in a lawn chair and brought her a cold beer. Blacky and Mutt, two cow dogs, arrived to lie by her feet.

Moments later, Ted rode through the trees into the yard. "Hey, boss. We need ya," he called.

Wasting no time for questions or explanations, Jeff swung up behind Ted and they galloped away. After commenting on his sudden departure, the rest of the family went on with the visiting, leaving Caly grateful for the company of the cow dogs.

She spent the entire afternoon drowsily watching the family from the safety of her lawn chair. No one went out of the way to exclude her, but they all hadn't seen each other for months, and were too busy catching up on the news to pay much attention to her. Caly sat and watched them and wished that she belonged.

Jeff's three sisters were all honey blondes, and looked so much alike that at first Caly thought they were triplets. It took her a while to realize that Mary Ellen and Bonnie Sue were twins about her age. Nancy Jane was thirty. Later that afternoon, Caly learned that Jeff had had an older brother, Stanley, Jr.

Mrs. Adams told her about Stanley, Jr. the only time she spoke to Caly that afternoon, describing haltingly how both he and his father had been killed in a small-plane crash on their way home from a rodeo when Jeff was eighteen. Her final words were, "Bill has been a big help, but I don't know what I'd have done if it hadn't been for Jeff. I depend on him for so much."

Each of the sisters later stopped by her chair and talked to her, and Caly learned that Nancy Jane and her husband, Brian McBain, owned an art gallery in Seattle and were the proud parents of Sarah, who was five, and Jennifer, who was four.

Mary Ellen and Russ Rashmusen owned a logging operation. Russ, an older man, was so shy that he didn't have anything to say to Caly. She wondered how he'd managed to ask Mary Ellen to marry him, but decided that it didn't matter. He obviously loved his wife and their four-year-old son, Rusty.

Bonnie Sue barely could wait to tell everyone her news. She and her husband, Michael Wilson, were expecting their first child in January. Brown-haired, browned-eyed Michael hovered around Bonnie Sue. Although both were outgoing and personable, at first Caly thought that they were too young to be owners of the Rendezvous Lodge. Then, from tidbits of conversation Caly overheard as the afternoon wore on, she realized that Jeff was part owner of the gallery, lodge, and logging operation. He obviously believed in looking after his family.

Caly knew that everyone was wondering about her, but only Sarah had the nerve to ask her anything about herself.

"Are you going to marry Uncle Jeff and give him babies?" Sarah demanded, peering up into her face.

"What?" That question startled her out of her drowsy state.

"My mother says that it's about time he got married again and had some babies." Popping the end of one of her braids in her mouth, she tightened the rubber band. "But when I asked Uncle Jeff if he was going to marry you, he just said he'd have to wait and see." She wagged a finger at Caly. "But he's been waiting for so very long, and he is going to be too old pretty soon."

Sarah skipped off before Caly could reply, leaving her to doze again.

Finally Babs announced that the steaks were ready. Caly walked carefully around the buffet table, taking only a small helping of salad and beans. Babs shook her head in concern, then piled one of the biggest steaks Caly had ever seen on her plate.

When she reached her seat again, she watched while Babs brought out her cake to place on the dessert table, and smiled at Caly encouragingly as she set it down.

Caly hoped that they would enjoy her cake, but when the family went through the line again, her hopes hit rock bottom. The apple pie and coconut cake disappeared quickly, but only Babs took a piece of her black forest cake.

Suddenly she had a crushing headache, like the ones she'd used to get when she lived with the Valemounts. If this was what a family picnic did to her, she was better off elsewhere. Maybe if she went down to the barnyard, she would feel more at home.

The cow dogs stuck to her like cheatgrass as she trotted through the barrier of Lombardy poplars and headed toward the corrals. She hoped Jeff would be there, but the yard was deserted except for a magnificent horse, which pranced across the corral to greet her. The red stallion looked as if he needed a run, and so did she—desperately. A saddle hung over the top rail, and she quickly saddled the restless horse. Minutes later they galloped across the range, the dogs at their heels.

The hot wind whipped her curls, making her feel alive again. She breathed deeply, and the tangy smell of sage helped to clear her mind.

As she rode she wondered what was the matter with her. She'd desperately wanted to be accepted by Jeff's family, but everyone had virtually ignored her.

Maybe it would've been better if Jeff had been there. Despite what she'd told him the other night, she would have appreciated his help. Where was her cowboy when she needed him? She wished he were riding beside her. They could stop under a big cottonwood tree and he could hold her and . . .

Mindful that she was a guest and that she had borrowed the horse without permission, Caly reluctantly turned the stallion around and headed back toward the ranch house. Although her headache had disappeared, her feelings of rejection and failure persisted. She wished she could keep on riding, away from everyone.

Spotting Jeff waiting by the corral, her spirits lifted, then were dashed again as she caught sight of his face. It was as black as a thundercloud.

"What the hell are you doing riding Firestorm?" Jeff shouted as they pulled up beside him in a cloud of dust. The wild bronc had just put his foreman in the hospital, and now Caly was riding him. "Get down from there!"

Firestorm, who'd been behaving like a gentleman, started living up to his name, and Caly quickly slid from his back, handing Jeff the reins.

"Yes, sir. Sorry, sir," she said, bristling.

Firestorm lunged at Jeff, then reared, pulling him off balance.

"Get out of here," he yelled at Caly, concerned about her safety.

Caly didn't hear the concern, just the words, and suddenly the tense wire that had been holding her together all day snapped, leaving her shaking. "Yes, sir. I'm going right away, sir. I can tell when I'm not wanted."

"What?" Jeff turned to look at her, barely dodging a flying hoof.

Halfway to the trees she turned and yelled at him, "I'm sorry I rode your horse. I'm sorry I took your dogs away from the party. But at least the animals made me feel welcome."

Ignoring his call to wait, she ran back to the party. Muttering unintelligible excuses, she picked up her unwanted cake and went home.

Seven

By the time Jeff reached Winthrop half an hour later, he was coiled tighter than his bull whip. He'd wanted to rush after Caly immediately but had been waylaid by his family. After explaining to his mother that Bill Stewart had been injured while trying to break Firestorm, he'd spent the next ten minutes reassuring her that the old fool would live. Then he'd grilled the others about what had happened while he'd been taking Bill to the hospital. Their disjointed explanations had left him with a sick feeling in the pit of his stomach. For the first time in his life he'd lost his temper with his family and in the process had made a few things clear—such as the fact that he loved Caly and was going to marry her.

If she'd have him.

He wasn't sure she'd even agree to see him. Doggone, he wished he'd been able to stay with her. She must have had a miserable time. And to top it off, he'd gone and yelled at her. But Lord, he'd almost died when she'd ridden up on that man-killer of a horse. Hell! He'd be lucky if she spoke to him again, let alone changed her mind about marrying him.

Zeke took one look at Jeff and ushered him into the kitchen, where Myra sat at the table.

"Can I see Caly?" Jeff asked the stern-faced Myra.

"She's upstairs."

Jeff swallowed hard. "Was she upset?"

"Very," Myra said dryly, making Jeff realize just how upset Caly must have been. Normally she hid her feelings well.

"Did she say why?"

"She mentioned something about the cake. That cake was very important to her."

He looked at the cake, which was sitting on the kitchen counter. It leaned over lopsidedly on the plate, whipped cream drooping down the side.

One piece was missing.

Myra continued to speak, her words biting into his core. "Caly got home at midnight last night and immediately started making it. Do you know how long it takes to make a black forest cake?"

He felt like crying. "Can I go up and see her?"

Myra's eyes and voice were very stern. "I don't hold with a man being in a young woman's bedroom. You won't be long, will you?"

"No."

Caly sat on the edge of the bed, polishing her silver heart-shaped locket. She wasn't crying, but her face was as white as the bedspread and her eyes were sunken-in blue hollows. She looked fragile and vulnerable and desolate.

"Hello, Caly," he said softly, and when she didn't respond, he asked, "May I sit down?"

She kept her head bowed, looking at the locket, but finally shifted over, giving him room at the foot of the bed. He sat down cautiously, turning his Stetson absently in his hands.

"I came to make some apologies, Caly," he said huskily.

She kept polishing.

"First, I'm sorry for what happened at the corral," he said.

There was dead silence except for the sound of soft cloth against silver.

"I know it's no excuse, but I was terrified that Firestorm would kill you. He's the reason Ted came running and I left in such a hurry. Bill, our foreman, decided to break him this afternoon, and got himself thrown and stomped."

Caly glanced up in concern. "Is he all right?"

"Yeah, but it looked pretty bad there for a while. I flew him over to Omak in the chopper. The doc says he's got a broken leg."

She lowered her eyes again. "I could've helped," she muttered. Her voice was lifeless, and again he had to fight down the overwhelming urge to hold her.

He swallowed hard, trying to ease the tightness in his throat. "I didn't think to ask. And I sure as hell didn't mean to yell at you. But when you came tearing into the yard on that damn stallion, all I could see was you crushed under his hooves, and I lost my cool. I'm sorry," he said, his voice hoarse with emotion.

She polished in silence for so long that he thought she wasn't going to answer. Finally she said quietly, "You worry about me too much."

"I can't help it."

"I know. You worry about all the women in your life, don't you?"

"Yeah, I guess so."

"Well, I'm not like the other women in your life. I'm not helpless and fragile." Slipping the locket over her head, she shook it under her shirt.

"Uh-huh." She was definitely fragile, but then wasn't the time to argue the point. She wasn't in the mood to hear his feelings on the subject. He gripped his hat brim to keep from touching her.

"I'd like to explain about the cake."

"There's no need. No one liked it." She stared resolutely at her hands, which were now clenched tightly in her lap.

She began whistling tunelessly. The sound tore at his heart, making him feel like crying again. He took a deep breath, but his voice was still husky when he spoke. "Mother is allergic to chocolate, so it's never been a big thing with the family. Besides that, we're pretty old-fashioned. We eat our fruit in a bowl and drink our liquor from a glass. That doesn't excuse the family, though, for not making you feel welcome."

She raised her eyes, and the misery in them stabbed his soul.

"It wasn't only the cake."

Unable to stand it any longer, he dropped the Stetson on the floor and gathered her into his arms, holding her carefully, as if she were one of his mother's china cups.

"I know, Caly, and I'm so sorry. I wanted today to be special for you. I wanted you to have fun and enjoy the family, and instead I deserted you and the family ignored you."

Caly leaned against him, but her body was still stiff. "It's obvious that they don't think I'm good enough for you."

His hand moved to her cheek, caressing it lovingly. "It wasn't you, Caly. They'd have acted the same way toward any woman I brought home. You just happened to be the first."

"Why?"

"They're afraid."

"Afraid! They couldn't have been more frightened than I was. What do they have to be afraid of?" she cried in anguish.

Raising her head, she glared at him fiercely, and he realized that she hadn't meant to say those words, hadn't meant to let him know how frightened she had been. Caly, who bragged that she was afraid of nothing, had dreaded meeting his family. But he knew if he pushed the issue now, she would deny it.

So he answered her question. "Of changes. Of what my loving you will do to their lives."

"If I were to marry you, Jeff, I'd never come between you and your family," she said earnestly.

"I realize that, and they'll also realize it once they know you better. If you give them a chance to get to know you, that is. It works both ways, Caly. Be honest, now. Did you really give them a chance today?"

He looked deeply into her eyes, daring her to answer him honestly.

"Oh, Jeff! You don't know how much I wanted to be accepted by your family. I've really never been part of a big family before, but I was so out of place in yours. I just knew that they wouldn't like me, and I was right."

Her eyelids drooped and her lips trembled, and she looked so sad that it almost broke his heart. He had to be strong, he told himself; he had to say a few more things that he knew might hurt her.

His voice was rough with emotion when he spoke. "Doggone it, Caly, you went to the picnic today with the idea that no one would like you. And what happened? You convinced yourself that no one liked you. They *did* like you, and they want to get to know you better, but you're ready to give up, aren't you? Before you have to take the risk of making friends with them." Unconsciously he gave her a gentle shake. "What happened to that brave tomboy I know who thinks nothing of taking on the world?"

She kept her eyes lowered as she thought about what he'd said. She had to admit that his words made sense, even though they didn't make her feel very good about herself. It was about time she stopped feeling sorry for herself. "She went into hiding," she said honestly, raising her gaze to his.

"Is she there to stay?"

"Nope," she said with renewed spirit.

"Good." He sighed in relief, then quickly pressed his advantage. "Then you'll come to the amateur rodeo at the ranch next Saturday?"

She hesitated a moment before taking his challenge. "All right, I'll come if I'm not out on a fire."

"You won't be."

Caly smiled at him then, and his heart did a slow turn. Lowering his head, he kissed her gently, intent on comforting her. Soon that wasn't enough, and he had to adore her, worship her, make love to her with his lips, his hands, his body.

"Oh, Caly, you don't know what you do to me," he murmured, raising his head and gazing down at her in wonderment. How had she gotten stretched out beneath him on the bed?

"I have a pretty good idea, all right, cowboy—exactly what you do to me." She smiled at him, her sherry eyes molten with passion, and he wanted nothing more than to be on her, in her, with her as they rode to the heights of love. Reluctantly he shook away the urge, trying to lighten the tension that tempted them.

"Good Lord, now look what you've made me do. Next thing we know, Myra will be up here with a shotgun."

He pushed himself away slowly but couldn't keep his eyes off her as she sat up and patted ineffectively at her curls.

"That definitely would be bad news, wouldn't it?" She grinned at him impishly.

An expression of sadness flitted across his face. "Not for the groom, but I'm afraid that the bride wouldn't be very happy. And the last thing I want is an unwilling bride." He managed a smile as he slid off the bed and picked up his Stetson. "Would you take pity on a poor cowboy and hold my hand while I try out a new experience—namely, eating a piece of your black forest cake?"

For a minute he was afraid he'd offended her; then

she laughed, and he felt relieved. He was making progress.

They entered the kitchen hand in hand, and Myra took a long look at them before nodding her head approvingly.

"There's a fresh pot of coffee on the stove. I thought it would go good with the cake."

On Monday the Smokejumpers who were left on base fought over the remains of her cake. Caly heard about it on Friday when she returned from a fire. The news did wonders for her ego, and she good-naturedly accepted their comments that she should stay home and bake them cakes for the rest of the summer.

Although she took more time than usual getting ready for the rodeo, she finally gave up in disgust. There was only so much you could do with unruly red hair. Jeff would just have to accept her the way she was. She felt quite sporty in a new pair of jeans and a blue-and-green plaid shirt.

Traffic was flowing steadily into the lower yards of the Half Moon Ranch when she arrived at noon. Ted, mounted on a restless chestnut, met her at the gate.

"Howdy, ma'am," he called, tipping his wide-brimmed hat. "The boss asked me to keep my eyes peeled for you. Follow me. I'll show you where to park that contraption."

Caly kept her contraption well back from the high-stepping horse as she followed it into the parking area marked "For Contestants." Parking her bike between a horse trailer and a motor home, she locked down her helmet and shifted her knapsack into a more comfortable position over her shoulder. Refusing Ted's offer of a ride, she walked beside him, skirting clumps of baby's breath and Barnaby's thistle as they made their way toward the fenced-in rodeo arena. It looked like a professional rodeo grounds, complete with bucking chutes, calf-roping chutes, holding corrals for the stock, and the announcer's booth, which towered over the arena.

Already people were spreading blankets and setting their lawn chairs up on the hillside overlooking the arena. A beer tent sat on the top of the hill, surrounded by the beer garden—if you could call a roped-off piece of mowed clover a garden. Nearby was a carnival-tent top surrounded by concession stands, which were doing a booming business.

"Here she is, boss. Lookin' mighty pretty," Ted called out.

Caly blushed as heads turned her way. Then people, noise, activity all faded as the green eyes of her Virginian caught and held hers.

"How are you?" he asked softly, taking her by the hands and searching her face carefully.

"Fine," she said breathlessly.

"Are you sure?"

"Wanna see how fine I really am?" Caly brushed her lips along his jaw, smiling as he sucked in a sharp breath.

"Behave yourself, Li'l Red," he said with a growl.

"Seems to me I remember a certain cowboy telling me to be brave."

"You're playing a dangerous game."

"And you like it."

Hearing a delighted laugh behind her, Caly turned to find Bonnie Sue watching them, along with five other interested spectators. Bonnie Sue, dressed in buttercup-yellow shorts, a T-shirt, and sun visor, looked pleased with herself and the world in general, but especially with her brother.

"Go to it." She winked at Caly. "I love it when my big brother blushes."

Laughing, Jeff reached down and pulled her blond pigtail, then slung his free arm across her shoulder while keeping the other one around Caly's waist. More people turned to smile at them.

A black buggy drew up beside them, driven by a gray-haired man sporting a cast on his right leg and Patricia on his left arm. Patricia, dressed in a pale blue denim skirt and a pink blouse and wearing a white hat, was definitely the queen of the day.

She leaned out of the buggy and told Caly softly, "I'm sorry for what happened last Sunday. We all are. We hope you'll forgive us."

Caly smiled at her and held out her hand. "There's nothing to forgive," she said as Patricia took her hand.

Her companion reached across Patricia and also shook Caly's hand. "So this is the gal who put me to shame." His gray eyes twinkled at her. "I'm Bill Stewart, the old fool. Mighty glad to meet ya. Heard a lot 'bout ya."

Caly laughed, delighted by the foreman's droll sense of humor. He was past retirement age, but that hadn't stopped him from trying to ride a bronc.

"Yes, you are an old fool," Patricia admonished Bill, tapping him on the arm with her program. "You should've been at the picnic with the rest of the family."

"I'm glad you're out of the hospital," Caly said, liking the way Bill smiled down at Patricia.

"Been telling the boss, here, he should give that red hoss to you, seeing as you're the only one who can ride him."

"I don't know about that," Jeff said gruffly.

Just then an announcement came over the loudspeaker that the rodeo would begin in ten minutes and that all contestants were required to ride in the grand parade.

"Sorry. I have to go," Jeff said, running his hand lightly up her arm.

"Are you in one of the events?" Caly asked absently, trying not to let on how much she was affected by Jeff's touch.

"Yep."

"Which one?"

"Tell you later. Stick close to Bonnie Sue, so I'll know

where to find you," he called over his shoulder as he loped across the field toward the corrals. The buggy followed.

"Come on. I have a blanket spread out, where we can sit," Bonnie Sue said, starting toward the hill.

"But that's for family."

"You're included."

Caly felt like skipping with joy, but shortened her stride to match Bonnie Sue's. Her boots kicked up the powder-fine dust, and she noticed that a water truck had just finished wetting down the arena.

"Where is everyone?"

"Michael is in the bareback event, so he's riding in the grand parade. Mary Ellen and Russ are checking in the contestants. Brian is busy slinging beer, and Nancy Jane is visiting with friends. Babs will be here shortly. Wild horses couldn't keep her away, especially when Jeff is riding. Here we are."

She flopped down on the huge Mexican blanket and reached for the ice chest.

"Want a cold drink?"

Crossing her legs, Caly sat Indian style beside her and accepted a soda. The sun beat down, and as she unpacked her camera she wished she'd worn a hat. She'd be as red as a tomato by the end of the day.

Babs arrived, panting. "Hello, Caly. Glad you could make it." She smiled wryly. "I really do mean it, y'know."

The parade began, led by four members of the Okanogan County sheriff's posse acting as flag bearers, carrying the American, Canadian, Washington state, and posse flags. The contestants followed, circling the arena before lining up two deep between the flag bearers. Next, the proud rodeo queens of five local rodeos showed off their horsemanship, waving and smiling as their horses galloped full tilt around the arena. Finally Bill drove Patricia around in style.

After the two national anthems came lengthy introductions. Caly clapped politely until the last introduction, then banged her hands together as Jeff took his bow. Remembering her camera just in time, she snapped his picture with the telephoto lens, catching him in the act of putting his black Stetson on the back of his curly-haired head.

Ceremonies over, Jeff and Michael ambled up the hill. Michael, who wore a shirt to match his wife's outfit, sat down beside Bonnie Sue and put his arm around her. Jeff stretched out beside Caly and smiled up at her. His smile turned to a frown.

"Here, you'd better wear this." He raised himself up on one elbow and plopped his hat on her head. "Can't have that cute little nose burned to a crisp."

She rubbed her nose and smiled at him, wanting desperately to lean down and kiss him. Their gazes met, and messages of desire passed silently back and forth between them. Finally Jeff looked away, reaching out to pick a blade of grass and stick it between his teeth. Caly forced herself to look at the arena, where the first event, team roping, was taking place. She watched in a happy daze, content to let the conversation flow around her.

When Jeff and Michael began talking about the horse Michael had drawn in the bareback event, she wondered idly what event Jeff was in. Picking up Bonnie Sue's program, Caly scanned it, finding Jeff's name on the last page, in the bull-riding event, paired with a bull called Cyclone.

"Bull riding!" she said. "You're crazy!"

Jeff glanced up at her in amusement. "Not as crazy as you are by riding that bike of yours."

"But it's dangerous!"

"No more dangerous than jumping out of airplanes."

"But at least I have a 'chute, and I won't get gored by a mean bull."

He chuckled, but there was no amusement in his voice. "What happens when you land in a tree? Don't you get gored then?"

"I've never yet been gored by a tree."

"And I don't plan to get gored by a bull, either."

Suddenly Caly became aware that the others were very interested in their lively exchange, so she shut her mouth. But she had a lot more to say. Bull riding!

An elderly couple sitting further down the hill waved at Jeff, and with a muttered excuse he went to talk to them.

Jeff had just rejoined them when Mary Ellen, Russ, Rusty, and the two girls arrived, and things became hectic for a while. When she wasn't distracted by the children Caly snapped pictures of Jeff with Sarah and Jennifer straddling his chest, of Jeff with Rusty sitting on his knee, of Jeff deep in discussion with Michael and Russ, of Jeff laughing with Mary Ellen and Bonnie Sue, and one more of him teasing Babs.

Although he was busy with the family, he touched her frequently as he explained the events and passed on tidbits about the competitors. He introduced her to everyone who stopped by to say hello to the family, making it very evident that he thought she was some-one special. As people smiled at them, Caly realized they thought Jeff was pretty special too. He was asked for his advice on breeding stock by an earnest young rancher, and thanked by an older man for helping him with seeding when he had been sick in the spring. Two children came over to tell him that the steer he had given them had won first prize in the calf show. A large, motherly-looking woman stopped by to remind him about a church-board meeting and added in an aside to Caly that Jeff had a beautiful voice and they were lucky to have him in the choir.

Michael disappeared to ride in the bareback-bronc event, coming back to receive their congratulations for his second-place finish. Then he wandered off toward the beer tent, and Caly saw him join Brian, who was still serving beer.

Partway through the barrel racing, Caly realized that

she and Babs were alone. Mary Ellen and Bonnie Sue had taken the children back to the house, and Jeff and Russ had wandered off.

"The family hates barrel racing, y'know," Babs said quietly.

"Oh?" She didn't know.

"I'm glad you aren't sore about what happened on Sunday. It would've tore Jeff to pieces if you'd stopped seeing him, y'know."

"Oh."

"They're a nice bunch, but Jeff's spoiled them rotten." She paused for a swallow of cola, then continued. "He's done a lot more for them than their father would've if he was still alive. But Jeff has always felt guilty because he's alive and Stanley, Jr. and his father are dead. The ranch was in pretty bad shape when Jeff took over, y'know, what with the money they'd been spending on small planes to fly all over to rodeos. But within five years he had it back on its feet and he—" She stopped, looking horrified. "I'm sorry. I don't normally talk so much, y'know."

"I know." Caly smiled at her reassuringly.

Babs eyed Caly thoughtfully. "Well, I hope he'll start thinking about himself for a change. He loves you, y'know."

"I know."

"Are you going to marry him?"

"I'm not sure." Caly dropped her gaze from Babs's face, fiddling unnecessarily with the lens cover of her camera.

"Well, I hope you decide yes. You'd be good for him."

Caly glanced up in surprise and embarrassment. "I . . . I'm nothing like what he needs in a wife. I can't even boil water."

"Hmm. For a woman who can't boil water, you sure whipped up a terrific cake."

"That was the first time I'd ever baked a cake," Caly admitted, smiling shyly at Babs's compliment.

"So Myra said." Babs continued. "I hope you won't mind my offering you some advice." She rubbed her nose with the back of her hand. "We women think we have to make fancy meals, but men like meat and potatoes best—at least Jeff does."

"I'm beginning to realize that."

"Mind you, it's up to us women to educate our men, but you have to do it kind of underhandedly, y'know."

Caly laughed, feeling certain she had made a friend. If she did marry Jeff, she knew that Babs would be her ally, teaching her the things her mother would have taught her if she had lived, and doing it in such a wise and humorous way that there would never be any hard feelings between them.

Babs must have felt the same way, because she reached over and patted Caly's hand as Jeff appeared.

"Regardless of what happens between you and Jeff, I hope we can be friends."

As Caly watched the tall, handsome cowboy approach, a deep feeling of contentment flooded through her. When he sat down beside her and draped his arm casually across her shoulder, she reached up and brushed a kiss across the corner of his lips.

He smiled at her, his eyes twinkling. "What's that for?"

"Nothing. Just an impulse."

"I like those kinds of impulses."

Bonnie Sue and Michael returned, arm in arm, and settled down on their corner of the blanket. They all teased one another and laughed for a few minutes, and then Jeff reached over and took his hat off her head.

"Guess I'd better borrow this back, Li'l Red. I should at least be wearing it when I come out of the chute."

Caly gripped his arm tightly, her amber eyes saying things she'd never have admitted out loud.

He caught his breath, then released it slowly. "How 'bout a kiss for luck?"

Hungrily she obeyed, kissing him the way she'd

wanted to all afternoon, with her lips open and full of fire. He returned the kiss, fueling her fire with his hunger, and when he finally raised his head, they were both trembling.

"Wow, you sure know how to shake up a cowboy, don't you? Is the competition paying you to distract me?" he asked huskily. Before she could answer, he scrambled to his feet. Jamming his hat on his head, he wove his way through the crowd of spectators and disappeared around the side of the arena.

Unable to sit still, Caly followed, crawling onto the top rail of a fence, out of harm's way but close enough to take pictures of the action. She snapped one as Jeff eased over the chute onto the back of the big white bull and worked his gloved hand under the bucking rope. He looked up, finding her unerringly as if drawn to her by some supernatural force. He smiled at her, and the force flowed between them, pulling them closer. Then the announcer asked if Jeff was ready, and he nodded at the man on the gate.

"Let'm loose."

The next eight seconds were the longest Caly had ever endured. Her heart flopped between her mouth and the pit of her stomach as the bull lunged out of the chute, twisting and turning one way, then throwing himself into a reverse spin. When that didn't dislodge his rider, he threw his belly up into the air, and Caly realized why he had been named Cyclone. How could anyone survive the ride?

Jeff was clamped on the massive beast like a vise, his free hand held high, his supple body rocking as he met each lunge and twist and dive. He was enjoying himself. Forgetting her fear, Caly began snapping pictures, catching the sheer guts and determination that kept Jeff aboard the sidewinder. And when the horn sounded, she captured on film his triumph at having topped the bull. Seconds later the pickup rider pulled him off Cyclone, depositing him on the ground by the chute.

Caly's yell of excitement turned to a scream of horror as Cyclone turned and charged his nemesis. Tossing his head, he slashed Jeff across the ribs with his horns as the cowboy swung up onto the gate.

Caly barely heard the announcer. "Well, ladies and gentleman, there's an old saying that the best comes last, and you've just seen it happen. The judges have awarded Jeff Adams an eighty-five for his ride on Cyclone. That's good enough for a first place in the bull-riding contest. Give the man a big hand, and let's also give him a hand for putting on another fabulous rodeo. That concludes . . ."

Frantic with worry, Caly jumped off the fence and ran behind the chutes, reaching Jeff as he crawled over the back fence.

"Are you hurt? Do you need a doctor? Oh, Jeff, you could've been killed."

With trembling hands she pulled at the rip in his shirt, exposing the raw, angry scrape that ran along the left side of his chest. It oozed blood—dark red blood. For a moment she felt dizzy, and from far off she heard Jeff's concerned voice.

"Caly. Are you all right?"

No, she wasn't all right. Jeff could have been killed, or gored so badly that he'd have spent months getting over it. How could he stand there smiling when he'd scared the living daylights out of her?

"Damn you, Jeff Adams. You said you never got gored. Another six inches and that horn would have gone through your heart."

He caught her hands and gave her a little shake. "I'm fine, Caly."

"But you're scraped. And you're going to be bruised."

"Caly, I'm okay. Really I am."

His words finally penetrated her panic, and she summoned enough control to give him a smile, but she couldn't stop the shudder that went through her.

Jeff smiled down at her, his eyes filled with love.

"Come on, let's go up to the house. I need a new shirt and you look as if you could use a drink." He pulled her against his left side, using her body as a shield against the curious gazes of the well-wishers who stopped him to shake his hand and congratulate him on his ride, or thank him for putting on the rodeo. Their progress was slow, and Babs, Bonnie Sue, and Michael caught up with them halfway to the house.

"Great ride," Michael said briefly.

"Thanks. Just lucky."

"Are you all right?" Bonnie Sue asked worriedly.

"Just fine, little sister. Now, don't you start worrying too."

"Caly, give Jeff a hand, will you," Babs said as they trooped into the kitchen. "I'll make coffee."

"The first-aid stuff's in here," Jeff said, leading the way down a short hall and into a utility room.

"Come here," he demanded, holding out a hand.

She flew into his arms.

Jeff had kept himself on a tight rein all day. Now he let go, releasing the passion and hunger he'd held in check. He captured her lips. His tongue blazed its way into the sweet cavern of her mouth, and he thrust, wanting to thrust elsewhere. It was torture, pure torture. Damn. He needed her. He ached with a fullness that wouldn't go away until he took her.

But he couldn't have her, not there.

"Lord, Caly." He rested his chin on top of her bowed head as he struggled to regain his breath. "What you do to me."

"I didn't do anything." She smiled into his chest, liking the totally masculine smell of him.

"It's hell having you so close and not being able to kiss you, touch you."

"You've been touching me all day."

"Not the way I want to."

He spanned her tiny waist with his large hands and lifted her easily onto the counter top, making a place for himself in the notch of her thighs. She caught him by the shoulders, wiggling closer, loving the feel of him against her.

"Did I tell you how beautiful you look today?"

She smiled. "No."

"This shirt's pretty." He undid the top button, then the second, folding the edges back to reveal the swell of her breasts. "But I like what's underneath better."

"Jeff, you shouldn't. Someone might—"

"Door's locked." He undid another button and another, then edged both hands inside to span her waist. Slowly his hands moved upward along her rib cage, thumbs in the center.

Caly sucked in her breath, wishing he'd hurry up and touch her breasts. They ached, and her nipples throbbed.

His thumbs slid under her breasts, lifting, supporting, molding the softness. She moaned as they rose from beneath her shirt, round globes held captive in his hands.

He bent his head. She tensed, waiting. His tongue brushed one nipple, then the other. Heat flashed through her. She wiggled closer, pressing her hands against his head.

He resisted her pressure, taking his time, touching her with his cheek . . . then his lips . . .

"Jeff, please!"

"Hmm."

His tongue flicked one taut peak, then the other. She gasped. "Shhh." He poised over a nipple, cooling its heat with the warm moistness of his breath. She trembled, wanting more.

When he finally took her nipple into his mouth, she gasped again, her body aching toward him. He sucked, pulling gently at first, then hungrily. While a part of her mind marveled at how he could give her such pleasure, the heat inside her grew and grew. Then all thoughts fled as his lips triggered a reflex that reached into her, drawing her, milking her. She shook as wave after wave of passion swept through her. When the glory was over, she collapsed in his arms.

He lifted a damp curl off her neck.

"Jeff, Jeff, what happened?"

"You went up like a flash fire."

She moved her head against his shoulder, trying to hide her embarrassment.

"But that's not supposed to happen."

"Maybe not with everyone, my Calypso." He chuckled. "But you're one hell of a woman."

"What . . . what about you?" she asked, straightening up to meet his eyes.

He grinned at her, looking pleased with himself. "I'll survive. I won't be fit for company for a few minutes, but it'll go away."

"Holy hat. What's everyone going to think?"

"That I love you." He hugged her again, then released her.

"But I'm supposed to be patching you up." She slid off the cabinet. Her knees felt like springs, and she wobbled. He caught her, holding her until her legs stopped trembling.

Finally he stepped back and, opening the cupboard door over the sink, removed a bottle of alcohol and a box of cotton swabs. She reached out and took the bottle from him. It slid through her trembling fingers, smashing to the floor.

Hands covering her mouth, she stared at him in horror.

"It's all right, Caly. It's just a bottle," Jeff said, bending over to pick up the big pieces of glass.

"No, it isn't all right," she whimpered. Visions of her grandparents' mansion and another bottle flashed through her mind. With them came all her old fears and insecurities. She would never fit in in his house, no matter how hard she tried. Jeff would want her to be the perfect wife, to be the perfect hostess to his friends, to be the perfect mother to his children. He wouldn't make a big issue out of it, but he would expect it of her. Even if she wanted to, she couldn't be perfect. She knew that from bitter experience.

She'd flounder around like a fish out of water and she'd continually do things to embarrass Jeff—and she'd wind up making his life miserable.

She had to get out, had to leave right away.

"Caly. What's wrong, honey?" He reached out to her. She shrank back against the door, fumbling with the buttons of her shirt.

As if in answer to her plea for help, someone knocked on the door.

"Hey, Caly, the base phoned," Michael said. "They want you there fast. Got a fire burning somewhere."

"Don't go, Caly," Jeff said sharply, unable to keep the fear out of his voice. "Call and tell them to send the next man on the list."

"I can't." She stuffed her shirt into her jeans and turned to unlock the door.

He caught her by the shoulder, turning her around to face him. "Why? Is it the money? Is that why you work day and night, seven days a week?"

She stared at him in shock, then realized that she still hadn't told him why fighting forest fires was so important to her.

She shook her head. "No. It isn't the money."

"Then stay."

"I can't, Jeff. They need me."

"And I need you too."

She felt the desperation in his hands, heard it in his voice. "I'm sorry, Jeff. I have to go," she said resolutely.

She did nothing to break his hold; she just stood there watching his face harden and his eyes become chips of ice.

"Go, then."

He released her, letting his hands fall to his sides. His wound was bleeding again, and Caly reached out.

He flinched away. "Don't touch me. I couldn't bear it."

She gazed at him for a moment, wanting to say something, anything, to make things better between them. But she couldn't say the words he wanted to hear. Blindly opening the door, she stumbled into the hall.

"Caly."

She turned back to him.

"Please take care of yourself," he said hoarsely.

She hadn't expected his reaction. Seconds before he'd been hurt and angry. Suddenly his face was full of fear and concern—and love.

She'd been able to withstand his anger, but not his expression of love.

She ran.

Eight

During the next three weeks the vision of Jeff standing in the doorway haunted her dreams. The hurt and disappointment in his eyes were bad enough, but the worry and fear she'd seen in his face troubled her even more. There was no way they could have any kind of relationship if Jeff was going to worry about her every time she went out on a fire—especially because he had good reason to worry.

She had taken care when she jumped the fire later that evening but had snagged up in a Ponderosa pine and had needed a climber pack, with its spurs, harness, and rope, to get down.

She'd been lucky. Pecos Bill had broken his leg landing in heavy deadfall, and Caly and the other two Smokejumpers had spent the rest of the night packing him through the heavy underbrush to an opening large enough for a helicopter to land and pick him up. It had meant leaving the fire, but the first priority on every jump was to ensure the safety of the fire fighters.

Many times during that night Caly had been thankful that she'd taken the medical-technician course. Bruises and sprained ankles were normal fare for

Smokejumpers, but broken bones were rare. As they loaded the injured man into the helicopter, she hoped Jeff wouldn't learn what had happened to Pecos. He'd have gone through the roof!

Two days later they'd been shipped out to California. The fire had been a wild one. She'd taken greater care than usual, but things had gone from bad to horrifying. The jump plane had crashed half an hour after they'd bailed out, and the next day a flaming torch had taken the pack off her back. Then the crew had been trapped in a canyon by a sudden wind change, and only another last-minute shift in wind direction had saved them from serious burns if not death. By the time the fire was under control, she was totally exhausted. At least she had a chance to shower and pick up a set of clean clothes before piling on the plane to fly back to the North Cascades base.

Zeke met them as they stumbled off the plane Friday evening.

"Take the weekend off, boys. I don't want to see you around here till Monday morning. If we need extra men, we'll bring in a crew from Redmond."

Caly stumbled toward her bike. All she could think of was taking a long soak in a hot tub and getting a good night's sleep.

Her plans evaporated like hail in a hot springs when she saw Jeff standing beside his Mercedes. Mindful of the onlookers she approached him slowly, pushing down her impulse to run to him and throw her arms around him.

"Howday, ma'am. Can I give you a lift home?" he said in his familiar drawl, his eyes caressing her. Looking into them, Caly felt as if she were drowning in the depths of her Emerald Lake.

She smiled at him, a dazzling smile that masked her tiredness. "I'd like that."

"Your carriage awaits you, ma'am."

With a bow, he opened the passenger door and helped

her inside. Caly sank into the chocolate-brown velour seat, thankful that she wasn't absolutely filthy and rancid with smoke, the way she usually was when she returned from a fire. Jeff didn't speak; he just kept looking at her as if she were pure gold.

Vaguely she realized that instead of going home, they were climbing into the mountains, but it didn't matter. All she wanted was to be with him.

The car turned off the main road and bounced along a trail that wandered through the trees. Once out of sight of the road, Jeff killed the engine and turned to her.

"Let me look at you." His hands framed her face, then moved across her shoulders and down her arms. Catching her hands, he turned them over, fingering a scab on her middle knuckle.

He looked up at her, his eyes dark with worry.

"I'm fine. Really, I am."

He grunted, then pulled her into his arms and held her against him. His body trembled, and he tensed trying to control it, but then he trembled again. Her hands went around him, running soothingly up and down his back.

"You're acting like a mother bear."

"I can't help it," he said, folding her closer. She felt enveloped—by his strong arms that held her close, by his broad chest that radiated heat, by his caring hands that caressed her head and her back, by the spicy scent of his after-shave lotion.

His lips nuzzled her neck, then worked their way along her jaw. She turned to meet them, and as his lips closed on hers she felt as if she'd come home at last. His kiss seemed to draw her into him, filling him, but filling her as well. When he finally raised his head, she was on fire, and she knew that her eyes must be shining with as much passion as she saw in his.

"Oh, Jeff . . ."

"I missed you," he said softly into her ear, pulling

her head down on his chest. "I started missing you the moment you left." His heart thumped wildly. "Why did you run, Caly? What did I do?"

The pain in his voice tore at her, making her want to weep. "I wasn't running from you," she whispered. "Just old memories that keep getting in the way."

"Tell me about them, Caly. Help me understand."

"Not tonight, please. I just want to be with you." She was too tired to deal with the memories or the pain they'd arouse. But she also wanted to do something about the agony of mind and spirit she felt in Jeff, something that would keep him from worrying about her. Running her hands down his flat stomach, she cupped him as she whispered, "I just want to please you."

"Caly," he said with a gasp, then pressed his pelvis upward.

"Be still." Feeling the rock-hard passion of him through the soft jeans, she caressed him lightly.

"Stop teasing, woman." He groaned and reached out for her.

"Be still," she warned again, pushing him back. He shifted his weight, leaning against the door, one leg stretched out on the bench seat, the other on the floor.

She laughed, wiggling around to kneel before him. Slowly she reached for his belt buckle.

"What are you doing to me?" he asked, holding himself stiffly, afraid to move. "More to the point, why am I letting you?"

"I want to pleasure you . . . the way you pleasured me."

It was the truth, but she also hoped she could make him change his mind about not making love to her while they were in the valley. No one would know.

She moved her hand, and he caught it, holding it still.

"No, Caly. Not here. Not now. Please, Caly. Don't tempt me." His voice was hoarse with emotion. "I desperately want to make love to you, but I wouldn't feel very good about myself afterward."

She sighed, giving in to his wishes. As much as she wanted to make love with Jeff, she couldn't force the issue if it meant that he would feel bad.

"I love you, my Calypso. I want to marry you." His hand moved against the nape of her neck, massaging away the tension there. "I want to be with you every minute of the day and night . . . I want you to hold me . . . to touch me . . . to make love to me." He dropped a light kiss on her head. "You pleasure me, my Calypso. You please me in every way."

She sighed, burrowing closer, soothed by his words. He continued to talk, telling her about his dreams of how they'd spend their life together. His voice gradually faded.

Jeff ran his hands along her shoulders and down her back, feeling her rib cage. She was so thin, so fragile, so exhausted. Every time he saw her she looked worse. She tried to hide it, to pretend that she was tough, but fighting fires was killing her. Slowly. Inch by inch.

More frightening yet, he'd learned from Zeke that she had almost been killed at least three times in the last three weeks. His stomach still felt sour whenever he thought about what had happened to her in California. His nerves were shot all to hell.

The next time out she might not survive.

Principles be damned. He didn't care what Myra thought, or the people in the valley, for that matter. He had to be with her, had to make love to her. He had thought he could wait, could take things slow and easy, could woo her with time and care. But he couldn't wait any longer. He had to convince her to marry him—fast, before he lost her.

"Caly, listen to me."

"Hmm."

"I can't go on like this much longer. I need to be alone with you. I need to talk to you, to be with you. To love you. Will you come away with me for the weekend?"

"Hmm."

It wasn't really a yes, but it would do. "Where do you want to go?"

"Home. To Emerald Lake. S'nice." She snuggled against him and drifted into a deep sleep.

He held her, feeling elated and frightened. What he was doing was wrong, and he didn't know if it would work, but he had to give it a try. He eased her back into her seat and looked down at her tenderly before starting the car.

She was sleeping so soundly when he arrived at the Olsens' that he was able to lift her and carry her into the house without waking her.

Myra met him at the front door and, noting his sleeping burden, waved him upstairs. After laying her gently on the bed, he sat watching her for a moment. She looked so young and defenseless, and he was filled with the urge to protect her.

"She's so thin," he said hoarsely to Myra, who was standing by the door watching them.

"She's had a tough three weeks."

"I know. I should've brought her straight home, but I just had to see her." He rose reluctantly. "Would you make sure she's up and ready to go by seven tomorrow morning, Myra? I'm taking her home for the weekend." He gave her a level look, asking for her understanding if not her approval.

Myra polished her glasses on her apron, put them back on, and peered at him, clearly undecided about whether she should be a part of this affair.

"I love her, Myra. She's the most precious person in the world. I know you don't approve, but we need to be alone. I can only promise that I'll do my darndest not to hurt her."

Myra nodded. "I'll see that she's ready by seven."

"Thanks."

With one last longing glance at the woman on the bed, Jeff left the room.

• • •

Caly could barely contain her excitement as Jeff landed the Bell Ranger in the clearing near the cabin she called home.

For the first time she realized the advantages of having money. Normally it took her two days to ride in on horseback. But Jeff had brought her there in less than two hours, and that had included a side trip over Washington Pass and a swoop around the majestic Liberty Bell.

Caly piled out of the helicopter before the blades had stopped turning. Once clear, she twirled around and around with her head thrown back. When Jeff appeared, she fell laughing into his arms. He caught her to him, kissing her soundly. Her camera dug into them, and she drew back, laughing again.

"It's great to be home. Let's go see the lake." Grabbing his hand, she led him across the meadow to the banks of Emerald Lake, which was cradled in the arms of three mountains she called the Three Wise Men. They towered above the lake, pine trees giving way to rocky peaks. Snow still clung in the shady ravines, and a glacier was draped like a dirty blanket over the shoulder of one of the mountains.

The lake was a shimmering tiara of blues and greens; starting with the pale green glacial water near the shallow shore, which turned to soft turquoise, then emerald, then sea green, and finally deep green along the mountain banks.

"It's beautiful," Jeff said, turning toward her.

"I'm so glad I can share it with you." She almost told him that his eyes reminded her of the lake every time she looked at him. They were such a deep green. So beautiful. She breathed deeply, trying to control the shaky feelings in the center of her being. "I've always dreamed of owning a dress that color." She laughed happily. "Of course, I'd never wear it, but I thought I'd take it out and look at it every once in a while."

He squeezed her hand and smiled at her gently, realizing that she was talking to cover up her feelings. She loved this lake and the mountains, and she also needed them. He didn't speak, giving her time to restore her soul, to fill herself with the beauty and peace that had been drained away by months of heat and fire. Finally, hand in hand, they walked slowly back to the cabin, stopping to watch three orange-and-black butterflies fluttering around a purple thistle. Much to Jeff's astonishment, one landed on the back of his outstretched hand. Caly snapped a picture.

"Hey, you'll break your camera."

"Don't make rude comments about my subject matter. I only photograph the best."

"You're silly. Are you sure you haven't been into the booze?"

"If I'm drunk, it's all your fault. You're making me giddy with happiness. Happiness at being here, at being able to share this with you."

She caught his smile in another picture, and then he was filling her viewfinder. And then he was kissing her.

He kept his kisses light and easy, sensing her need to play awhile. Finally they wandered toward the cabin, mellow with happiness.

Nailed to the door was an official notice informing the occupant to vacate by September first.

She no longer had a home.

"Good Lord, Caly, what does this mean?" Jeff asked, ripping the notice off the door.

She barely glanced at it. "I've been expecting it. Big Red built the cabin long before there were any restrictions, and he was allowed to keep it because he worked with forestry." She shrugged. "Now that he's gone, I guess they've decided to enforce the law."

Angrily Jeff balled up the notice, started to pitch it, then stuffed it in the back pocket of his jeans. "What are you going to do? Where are you going to go?" He desperately wanted to ask her to marry him, to tell her that she would always have a home with him—but he knew better. She wouldn't marry him simply because she needed a home.

"Don't worry, I'll find a place to hang my hat. Let's open up, shall we?" She sounded casual, but Jeff knew she had to be hurting inside.

Walking around the cabin, they unlatched the two shutters and propped them open.

"I'm surprised that the cabin hasn't been vandalized," Jeff said, brushing his hands clean on the sides of his jeans.

"It's too far off the beaten track." Caly used the seat of her jeans for the same purpose.

"Thank goodness you won't be staying here this winter."

Caly smiled at him but also shook her head in warning. "There you go again, worrying needlessly about me." Reaching into a nook under the low eaves, she found the key and opened the door. "I've never been afraid, even when Big Red was away hunting."

"You're too trusting."

"No, siree. I have a sturdy door and a good rifle. Come on inside."

The cabin smelled stale, but all it needed was a good airing and they could sleep inside that night. Caly was pleased. She wanted to make love with Jeff in her bed, the bed that had been her parents'. The bed where she'd been born. The bed that she'd used since she'd come home from the Valemounts'. There were so many memories in the cabin—some happy, some sad—and she wanted Jeff to be part of them.

She turned to find him gazing around the room in astonishment.

"I know it isn't much," she said, half in apology, then stopped. Why should she be apologizing because she'd spent her life in a one-room cabin that was heated by a wood stove and had outdoor plumbing? Her mother had been happy there, despite the fact that her only privacy had been the bear-hide curtain that screened her bed from the rest of the room. Her mother had never longed for the luxuries of her childhood home— and Caly had hated them.

"Not much! They're terrific." He noticed her confusion. "I'm talking about the pictures. Did you take them?" he asked, referring to the framed photos that covered the walls.

She nodded, embarrassed by the abundance of pictures, and felt the need to explain. "Big Red did the developing, enlarging, printing, and framing. The silly man would've hung every photo I took, so I finally had to put down my foot and insist that he only keep the best ones."

She held her breath, waiting for his reaction. Big Red had thought they were all terrific, but of course he was biased. She figured some of them were pretty good, but she didn't really trust her judgment.

The shock of watching her grandfather destroy all of her mother's drawings still affected her after so many years. She'd loved her mother's drawings and had been grateful that Big Red had sent most of them along with her when she went to live with the Valemounts. But when Grandfather Valemount had seen them, he'd called them trash and had burned them. As much as she'd hated her grandfather and mourned the loss of her mother's drawings, she still had no confidence in her judgment. Or in her own work.

Jeff's reaction left her with no doubts about what he thought. "These are fabulous, absolutely fabulous."

She let her breath out in a pleased sigh. He liked them!

"Big Red gave me my first camera when I was eight, an old Brownie. In fact, that picture over there was on my first roll."

It was a black-and-white picture of a lookout tower that had been partly burned. It told its story in a glance. Jeff pointed at the next one, showing the head and paw of a black bear eating dark red raspberries.

"How did you get so close?"

"That's Old Blacky. He's harmless."

"He doesn't look harmless, but you have a way with animals, don't you?" He smiled at her sheepishly.

One by one he studied the pictures, while Caly told him when she had taken them and why each was special. She chatted along happily, pleased to be able to share her life with Jeff, and he asked probing questions that filled in the gaps. Here, then, was the other half of the mystery that was Caly, he thought.

He couldn't tell her what he saw in her pictures. She wasn't ready to hear it. She still thought she was a rough-and-ready tomboy. But Caly was no tomboy; she was a brilliant, sensitive woman who had a special talent that most professional photographers would have given their darkrooms to possess. She made the viewer taste, smell, and feel the picture, actually experience it. She had a rare gift, and she didn't know how good she was. And he knew she wouldn't believe him if he told her.

Breaking out of his reverie, he realized that Caly had moved over to the bed and was staring down at two framed pen-and-ink drawings that sat on the wooden apple box that served as a bedside stand. The look on her face tore a hole in his heart.

"Are these yours?" he asked softly, walking over to stand beside her.

"My mother drew them." Thank goodness Big Red hadn't been able to part with them when he'd sent her to the Valemounts.

Sitting down on the bed, Jeff picked up the pictures. One was of a curly-headed toddler, obviously Caly, playing with two wolf cubs. The other was of a tall, laughing man, dressed in the garb of a Smokejumper.

"I'm not an expert, by any means, but I'd say your mother had real talent. These drawings are exceptional."

Slowly Caly's face lit up in a smile. Her eyes stung with thankful tears. His praise of her mother's work meant more than his comments about her photos.

"I've always thought so, but I didn't know for sure. It's good to have someone else confirm my feelings." She sat down beside him and took the drawing of the man out of his hand.

"Is that your father?"

"Yes."

"I can see why you wanted to be a Smokejumper. Do you have a picture of your mother?"

Laying her father's picture on the apple box, she pulled the silver locket over her head and flicked it open. The colored miniature inside was of a beautiful woman who looked like a brown-eyed Susan, with her golden hair and brown eyes.

"She was beautiful."

Caly nodded, then snapped the locket shut and dropped it over her head.

Replacing Caly's picture on the stand, he brushed a tender hand along the side of her sweet, stubborn jaw, and raised her chin so he could see her eyes. They were full of sadness and pain and memories. Although he'd asked, she'd never shared those memories. He hoped this time she would.

"You once told me that your parents died when you were seven. What happened to you? Did Big Red take care of you?"

She leaned her head against his chest and mumbled, "I went to my other grandparents, the Valemounts, for a while. They lived in Kansas."

"You didn't like it there." It wasn't a question—he had heard the pain in her voice.

"No. It was flat country, and I was homesick for the mountains."

He had a hunch that wasn't the real reason she didn't like living with her grandparents. Somehow he had to make her tell her story; otherwise it would always be there, haunting them.

"So they let you come home?"

She didn't reply immediately, and when she started to whistle tunelessly, Jeff realized he'd been right. He pulled her closer, trying to comfort her.

At last she spoke, her voice husky with emotion. "Not right away. They were very strict, you see, and thought that it was their duty to give me a proper upbringing."

His arms tightened convulsively, then loosened, holding her tenderly.

"Duty! Didn't they love you?"

The anguish in his voice broke the ice around her heart. The glacier that had held her emotions prisoner melted, and the words flowed.

"I don't think they knew how to love anything but money. They lived in a big house and had lots of servants and furniture and everything. But I hated it there. It was so cold." She shivered, and Jeff rubbed her back, trying to ease the tension that knotted her muscles. After a few deep sighs she continued. "My mother must have thought so, too, because she ran away from home when she was eighteen. They never forgave her, and the only reason they knew about me was that Big Red sent me to them. He wanted to keep me but thought they could provide a better life for me."

She shivered again as she remembered how unhappy she'd been. She had felt totally deserted, certain that no one wanted her or loved her. First her parents had left her, and then Big Red had sent her away.

Jeff's hands moved soothingly in her hair, and she stumbled on, feeling relieved finally to be able to talk it out.

"They burned her pictures, you know. Grandfather said they were no good."

Jeff's hand paused, but he didn't say anything. He was afraid he might blow sky high.

"They didn't like anything about me either," Caly continued. "I was too skinny. My hair was too red. I didn't know how to talk correctly, and I used the wrong fork. I stumbled over their rugs and broke a big old bottle that had dragons on it." She paused for a moment, remembering another bottle she'd broken recently.

Jeff remembered too. "Oh, Caly," he said breathily, holding her closer.

She rushed on with her story. "They were ashamed of me, so they set out to change me into a perfect little girl who had perfect manners and did everything perfectly." Her voice dropped to a whisper. "I'm afraid I wasn't too cooperative, and I spent a lot of time locked up in the closet in my room."

"How could they?" He felt like beating the tar out of the old man, but at the same time he felt like crying. No wonder she was afraid he'd try to change her.

She looked up at him, a smile trembling on her lips. "I realize now that they were only doing what they thought was right. Or at least what Grandfather felt was right. Grandmother went along with him." She sank back against him with a sigh, staring unseeingly at the patchwork quilt her mother had made.

"What happened?"

"Big Red came for a visit and found out what was going on."

"So he took you home."

"Not right away. He had to fight a court battle first." She shuddered, and Jeff rocked her, crooning softly. "I remember being so frightened because I overheard Grandfather Valemount say that he'd use every last cent to keep me away from Big Red. Afterward Big Red told me that the only reason he won custody was that I clung to him and wouldn't let him go. Apparently it made a big impression on the judge."

Tears stung Jeff's eyes, and he blinked them away. "Thank God," he whispered huskily, swallowing against the tightness in his throat. "What happened to them?"

She looked up, her eyes full of sadness, but she managed to give him a misty smile. "I don't know.

They disowned me, said they didn't want Big Red getting his hands on their money. As if we wanted it, or needed it."

Pulling out of his arms, she slipped off the bed. She prowled around the room, and Jeff could sense her determination to become once again the tough, independent tomboy who needed no one in her life. He felt helpless and frightened. If the barriers went up, would they ever come down again?

He dug his fingers into the edge of the mattress in a desperate attempt to prevent himself from going after her. She would have to come to him of her own free will.

"You're right, Caly. You don't need the Valemounts, and you don't need me," he said hoarsely. She turned to look at him, drawn by the pain in his voice. "But please, Caly, let me love you. Let me cherish you. Let me take away your hurt and help you believe in love."

His compassion flowed across the room to surround her, seeping into her like the warmth of the summer sun. This man, her Virginian, knew so much about love, about giving, that he could make her believe in him and almost believe in herself.

"Please come to me, Caly. Let me love you."

Slowly she walked across the room. He held out his arms to her. They trembled. Tears shone in his brilliant eyes. Seeing them, she flew the rest of the way into his arms.

"Oh, Jeff. How can you love me?"

"It's very easy, my Calypso. Let me show you."

He lowered her to the quilt and leaned over her. Her eyes were wide open and vulnerable, making him realize how much she trusted him. He felt humble and grateful and afraid.

Light from the window fell on the bed, spinning her hair into a cobweb of burnished copper. Lord, she was so beautiful! he thought.

He sucked in a deep breath, realizing what he had to do and praying he would find the right words.

"I'm just a cowboy who's not used to talking about how he feels, my Calypso. But what I'm about to say is the truth, and I won't let you or anyone else call me a liar. Is that understood?"

She nodded, a frown of puzzlement marring the smooth skin of her forehead.

"The truth is that you are a very beautiful lady, and I don't want to change one single, solitary thing about you." He said each word slowly and distinctly.

"What?"

"Shhh." His finger covered her lips, but it was his look that silenced her. He really did think she was beautiful.

His hands moved to her head, his fingers gently lifting her curls. "I love your hair. It's the color of flames, and with the sun shining on it, the way it is now, everything around you glows with warmth and life." His voice grew husky. "I can never get enough of touching it, but I want to touch all of you."

His hands framed her face as his lips touched each eye. "I'm not a drinking man, but when I look in your eyes, I'm reminded of brandy, the rare kind, the kind that makes a man feel light-headed and happy and, oh . . . so good."

Caly sucked in her breath as she saw the adoration in his eyes. A warm glow was starting somewhere in the region of her heart.

He dropped a kiss on the tip of her nose. "I hope all our daughters inherit your sassy little nose. It makes a man feel happy, just looking at it."

Her lips quirked, his light humor making her feel good.

"But your mouth. Ah, that's different. It makes me want to cherish you." He lowered his lips to hers, kissing them tenderly, sweetly, giving her all his love and caring. "Worship you . . ." His lips gave her more—all of him—and the band around her heart began to loosen, the tightness in the rest of her body to ease. "Adore you . . ." Suddenly all barriers were gone and a feeling of contentment seeped into her soul.

She lay there, eyes closed, so cherished that she wasn't the least bit concerned when he raised his head. She knew that he was removing her shirt, but that didn't matter. She could feel his eyes on her breasts, but that didn't matter either. She felt different, somehow, like a sensual cat, and she gloried in the knowledge that a man—no, her cowboy—found her body beautiful.

He was silent for so long that she finally opened her eyes. The look on his face made her bones melt with longing.

"Jeff . . ." She reached up for him.

"Shh, my Calypso. Lie still. I want to worship you." His hands brushed her aching breasts, then kneaded them, shaped them. "You're all woman. So perfect." His voice was almost a whisper. "I want to see our child nursing here."

His lips covered her nipple, pulling gently, then sucking deeply. Shafts of pleasure passed through her to the core of her being. She gasped, digging her fingers into his hair.

Jeff no longer spoke, but his moans told her more than any words. He wanted her. He desired her. He thought she was beautiful—and she was beautiful.

She was shaking when he finally raised his head, and the heaviness in her lower body was more than she could bear.

"Jeff. Please . . ."

"Not yet, my Calypso, but soon. I promise." His words came out in short gasps, and he took a deep breath to regain control. "I haven't finished adoring you yet."

With trembling hands he slid her jeans and panties down her legs. She watched his eyes travel the length of her, then back, and she opened her legs slightly, moving her hips enticingly. He didn't touch her with his hands, but his eyes caressed every part of her as he whispered huskily, "Your legs drive me to distraction. They're so long and sexy, and I keep thinking of how they feel when they're cinched around me. But I think of you when you're walking in the forest, too, and how graceful you are, how lithe and easy and free. You walk the way a woman should walk, not like some prissy high-society gal. You walk like my kind of gal."

"Oh, Jeff . . ."

"I can't take any more, my Calypso. I want to spend the rest of the day looking at your beauty, but I can't. I have to make love to you. Now."

He shed his clothes quickly, then spent a moment taking care of her before nudging her legs open. Unable to wait any longer, she moved against him. And then they were one.

"Ah, my sweet, sweet Calypso. Heaven."

She moved again.

"No. You can't have me. Not yet. I want you to feel me loving you. All of you."

He filled her. Totally. Then withdrew. Then filled her again. His body worshiped her, adored her, filled her with love. His love seeped into every part of her being, and she no longer fought it. She believed. And, believing, she let go of all her doubts, fears, and unhappiness. She was loved.

Her climax, when it came, chased the shadows from her soul, leaving her open and vulnerable—but unafraid.

Holding his trembling body above her, Jeff looked down into her eyes. They were luminous with love.

"That—that was so beautiful, I . . ." She blinked back happy tears.

He laughed in pure pleasure, then rolled off her, gathering her into his arms. Over the pounding of his heart and his labored breathing, he heard the mountain bluebird singing outside the open window. It was a beautiful day.

"Are the ghosts gone?" Jeff asked when he could finally speak again.

"Yes, Jeff. The ghosts are gone." She sounded happy, and her happiness made his complete.

"Good. And you believe that I love you and that I don't want you to change?"

"I believe you."

He lay there, holding her while their bodies cooled and their breathing steadied. His hand gently soothed her back as he looked over her shoulder at the pictures on the wall. What a childhood she'd had. No wonder she was afraid he wanted to change her. But he didn't, he knew; he just wanted to marry her.

And then he realized that despite his words, he did want her to change. He wanted her to give up the most important thing in her life—fighting fires. And she wouldn't, unless she decided that she loved him more.

She still hadn't told him that she loved him.

It was almost noon when Caly awoke from a deep, refreshing sleep. For the first time in her life she felt at peace with herself and with the whole world. She owed the wonderful feeling to Jeff, to the very special cowboy who gave and gave and gave of himself.

Careful not to disturb him, she sat up and gazed at him. He lay on his stomach, with his head turned toward her. He looked so adorable that she could hardly keep from touching him. She felt like a little girl in a pet shop who wanted to take home a puppy but knew she couldn't. No, she couldn't take Jeff home with her, but she could take his picture. She could capture this feeling, this moment, and take out the picture and look at it when the going got rough.

Easing herself out of bed, she padded across the log floor to her camera bag. Making the necessary adjustments to the settings, she returned to the bed and snapped a picture. The flash roused Jeff. He raised himself up on his elbow, looking so sleepy and lovable that her heart turned over in a slow loop and settled in the pit of her stomach. She snapped another picture.

"Come back here, my Calypso." He reached out a hand, smiling at her with a lazy, sexy smile. She released the shutter again.

"I don't like the look in your eyes, Caly. What are you thinking?" he said with a growl, catching her by the arm and pulling her down on the bed. She dangled the camera onto the floor, then rolled over to straddle him, pinning his wrists with her knees.

"That you'd make a terrific centerfold for *Playgirl*." She wriggled against his chest, delighting in the feel of his hair against her softness.

"You wouldn't dare!" He raised his head. "How do you know about such things?"

She laughed huskily. "Just because I've lived in the bush all my life doesn't mean I'm totally ignorant."

"Prove it, my Calypso. Prove it."

It was much later before they dressed and took Jeff's picnic basket outside to eat under a tamarack tree. Babs had packed fried chicken, potato salad, and cole slaw, and Jeff had brought wine.

"Mmm, this is delicious," Caly mumbled with her mouth full of chicken. "I don't know what's the matter with me. I'm starved."

"Are you pregnant?" Jeff looked at her with a hopeful expression on his face. "The last time we talked about it you said it was too early to tell."

She waved the chicken leg at him, trying to cover her embarrassment. "Don't worry, I'm not eating for two. I'm just trying to make up for a few missed meals."

"You're sure?"

"Positive."

"Damn. I'd like nothing better than to be married to you and have a houseful of kids with curly red hair."

She pictured Jeff playing with a redheaded girl and boy, then added a couple of boys with black hair and beautiful green eyes for good measure. Realizing what she was doing, she brought herself up short. She hadn't even said she'd marry him, and there she was, dreaming about his children.

"A houseful! How many is a houseful?" she asked in confusion.

His eyes danced. "Hmm, let me see. At least a dozen. Once we start making them, you'll have a hard time stopping me."

"A dozen!" she cried.

"Well, I guess I'd settle for half that number." He tousled her hair, chuckling softly. Then he was serious again. "I'll try to take care of you this weekend, Caly. But if anything happens, promise that you'll tell me. I would never want a child of mine to be a bastard."

"I promise," Caly said softly, meaning every word. He nodded his thanks, then looked away.

They finished their meal in silence, with Jeff obviously brooding about something and Caly watching him thoughtfully, taking a picture now and then.

"Caly," he said. "I . . . would you—"

Caly quickly placed a finger over his lips, silencing him. She knew what was coming and felt panicky. She didn't want this time with him to be spoiled because she'd hurt him. She wasn't ready to say that she'd marry him, despite everything that had happened between them since they'd arrived at Emerald Lake.

"Don't ask. Not yet."

He sighed. "I can't wait much longer."

"Please. Let's just have fun today. I need a day of fun."

He studied her carefully, taking in the signs of fatigue and strain. "Yes, you do, don't you? You need fun and laughter and love, and that's what I'll give you."

They did have fun: swimming in the lake; sunning and making love on the grass; walking in the woods; making love under the trees; eating supper over a campfire; and making love again.

For Caly it was a time of laughter, but more importantly it was a time for recharging her soul, drawing from the beauty around her and from the strength and goodness of the man beside her.

For Jeff it was a time for nurturing, for giving Caly the love, the tenderness, and, above all, the freedom she needed to flourish.

At the end of the day, they wandered back to the lake to watch the sun set on the Three Wise Men. The peaks glowed like molten gold, then deepened to a rosy red against the backdrop of a sky that turned from silver blue to azure, then to dark indigo.

Jeff sat on a log, spellbound by nature's brilliant handiwork, oblivious to the fact that Caly was snapping pictures of him. It was the most beautiful sunset he'd ever seen, and he couldn't remember when he had ever felt as contented and happy.

Then he remembered that, despite all the loving they'd done, Caly hadn't said the words he longed to hear.

Nine

"Today is D-day. Today is D-day." Caly woke the next morning with the phrase echoing in her mind.

Jeff was going to ask her to marry him. She'd have to make a decision—and she wasn't ready to do that.

She'd been so busy fighting fires that she'd had no time to think, no time to sort out her feelings, let alone find herself.

Jeff stirred in his sleep, and, rolling her head, she looked at him. He was so tired. The strain of worrying about the drought—and worrying about her—had taken its toll. She thought about the previous day and how he had cared for her, given her his strength, his love, his courage . . . when he was in need of comfort too. He was such a good man, and it would be so easy to agree to marry him. . . .

Realizing where her thoughts were leading her, she slipped carefully out of bed, dressed, and hurried down to the lake.

It had always provided her with solace in the past, and, sitting on her favorite log, she stared out at the beauty around her, hoping that it would give her some answers.

There was no question in her mind that she loved Jeff. She'd loved him since he'd brought her the Calypso orchids. The question that kept her in a turmoil was: How could she marry him and keep the promise she'd made so many years ago?

She wanted to marry him, but he'd insist that she give up fighting fires, and she couldn't do that. She couldn't break the vow she'd made on her parents' grave. She'd feel so guilty. They had been two very loving people, and it wasn't fair that they had died so young. The only way she could honor their memories was to fight what had destroyed them.

Dammit. Why did it have to be so hard? Why did she have to hurt Jeff—because that was what she was going to do when she told him, as she must, that she couldn't marry him?

Caly dropped her aching head to her knees. Never before had she felt so tired. She'd been physically exhausted many times, especially during fire season, but she was emotionally exhausted, too, something that had never happened before.

Now her love for Jeff was tearing her apart.

Raising her head, she stared at the lake again. Lost in the misery of her thoughts, she didn't hear Jeff until he was standing beside her, holding a steaming mug in each hand.

"How's my beautiful Calypso this morning?" he asked, kissing the tip of her nose before handing her one of the mugs. She tried, but the smile didn't reach her lips, and she shivered slightly.

"What's the matter, love?"

"I'm cold."

Sitting down beside her on the log, he placed his free arm across her shoulder. His blue shirt wasn't buttoned, and she could feel the warmth of his body. She leaned against him gratefully, drawing heat from him and from the mug she cradled in both her hands. He waited until she drank some of the hot coffee before he asked again.

"Why so sad?"

Caly took another sip of her coffee. She knew she should tell Jeff how she was feeling, but she wanted to delay it as long as possible.

"I've been thinking that I should spend today packing," she said finally. At least it was one of the reasons she was feeling so sad.

Jeff squeezed her shoulder.

"Leave it. I'll send Ted in to pack your things and send them down to you."

This time the smile came, but she still looked sad. Draining her coffee, she put the mug down beside her on the log.

"Thanks. That's a big relief. I thought I'd have to take time off so I could move out of here before September."

Suddenly Jeff was kneeling in front of her on the grass, gripping her arms. "Marry me, Caly. We can get the license tomorrow and be married in forty-eight hours, and you can stop being a Smokejumper. I can't stand the thought of your going out on another fire," he said hoarsely. Sinking to the ground, he wrapped his arms around his bent knees to keep from shaking. "I can't lose you too."

She heard the pain and desperation in his voice. " 'Too.' What are you talking about?" she asked, kneeling beside him.

"Betsy was just riding in a barrel race," he muttered, staring blindly at the lake, refusing to look up as Caly put a tentative hand on his elbow.

"I don't understand."

"It's a long story, one I'm sure you don't want to hear."

She was afraid she already knew what had happened to Betsy, but she needed to hear it from Jeff, despite how much the telling would hurt him.

"But I do. It's the reason you're so worried about me, isn't it?" she asked, reaching for his hands.

"Uh-huh."

"Then don't you think I deserve to know what happened?" she insisted, finally succeeding in unclasping his hands so she could hold them in her own.

Slowly he turned his head and looked at her. "You know that I married my childhood sweetheart." She nodded, willing him to go on. When he did, his voice was so soft, she could barely hear him. "Well, Betsy was killed riding in a barrel race at the Spokane Rodeo." He chewed on the corner of his lip until Caly was afraid that he'd make it bleed. She touched his lips, and he stopped chewing, then drew in a ragged breath. "She was an excellent rider, but she broke her neck when her horse fell. One minute she was laughing. The next she was dead."

Caly slipped her arms around Jeff and pulled him close. For a moment he resisted, then relaxed against her.

"I'm so sorry, Jeff. I didn't know." No wonder he worried about her, she thought.

He clutched at her. "I can't risk losing you too. Not after waiting all these years to find you. I love you, Caly. I want a wife, not another grave marker."

Jeff began trembling, and as Caly held him, she watched his face tighten with pain. All his defenses were down, and he made no effort to hide his vulnerability. And she was the reason for his feeling vulnerable. He loved her, and the fear that he might lose her was eating away at him like a root fungus and would eventually destroy him.

The knowledge strengthened her resolve. She couldn't do that to him. She had to end things immediately.

"I'm sorry, Jeff," she repeated, feeling lower than a slug because of what she was about to do to him.

"Then you'll stop fighting fires?" His face filled with relief, and his eyes shone with hope. Caly couldn't bear to look at him any longer. Dropping her arms, she rose to her feet.

"I can't," she choked out.

"Can't what?" he demanded, pushing himself upright to stand behind her. "Can't stop fighting fires, or can't marry me?"

"Both."

Suddenly he was angry, and hurt, and totally frustrated. He felt like grabbing her and shaking her, but as his hands caught her shoulders, he stopped. She was so thin, so fragile, and the last thing he wanted to do was hurt her. He dropped his hands.

"Why?" he demanded hoarsely. He'd reached the end of his emotional rope, and he desperately needed answers.

She heard the desperation in his voice and knew that he, too, deserved an explanation. She turned around, deliberately keeping her feelings from showing on her face.

"I have to. My parents were killed in a forest fire."

Her stark words erased the last of Jeff's anger. He reached out, wanting to comfort her. When she pulled away, he felt helpless and sick at heart.

"What happened?" he asked softly.

There was still no expression on her face, and her voice was devoid of emotion as she plowed through the explanation. "They also died in a flukey accident. Dad wasn't even fighting a fire when it happened. The three of us were spending the day in the woods over there." She waved across the lake. "Mom was drawing, Dad was sleeping under a tree, and I was watching ants a few feet away. A storm rolled across the mountain, and lightning struck the tree near Dad. It exploded into flames, and a burning limb fell on him, staking him through the chest." She swallowed hard, trying to ease the tightness in her throat. "Mom ran to help him and got there just as the top of the tree crashed down on them."

Once again Jeff stepped toward her but she backed away, knowing that if she let him touch her, she wouldn't be strong—and she needed to be strong.

She squared her shoulders and looked at him with sad, determined eyes. "So you see, I have to fight fires. A fire will never destroy another human being if I can help it."

Jeff raked his hand through his hair, wanting to shake her.

"But that's crazy."

Her eyes flashed. "I made a vow, and I have to keep it."

"But that's unreasonable. You can't fight fires for the rest of your life."

She lowered her eyes, and Jeff's heart sank.

"You don't think you're going to live very long, do you?"

Her lack of an answer confirmed his horror.

"You're not thinking straight, Caly." He took a deep breath, trying to calm down. He realized that she was in no condition to listen to reason, but he had to try. If he didn't say something then, he would never get another chance. Caly was preparing to walk out of his life.

"I can understand why fire-fighting is so important to you. I can see why a child would make such a promise and keep it." He passed a trembling hand over his face. "But you're a woman now, Caly. Surely you can't believe that your parents would be happy if they knew what you were doing. They'd want you to get married, raise children, have a normal life. Not fight fires."

She hadn't thought of it quite like that before. "Maybe you're right—I don't know. But it's the only way I know to honor them . . . honor their memory."

"You could do that with your photos."

"I'm not good enough."

"I think you are. You have a rare talent, Calypso Robbins, and you're not using it. You could do a lot of good with your photos."

She wrapped her arms around her chest, trying to

hold herself together. She felt as if she were being torn apart.

"I don't know, Jeff. I—it's too much to think about."

He enfolded her in his arms. "Marry me, my Calypso," he whispered into her hair.

"Oh, Jeff. I"m so confused." She covered her mouth with her hand, her eyes dark with turmoil. "I want to marry you, truly, I do. But I need more time to think, to sort things out."

"How much time, Caly?"

"I don't know. When I'm on the fire lines I don't have time to think, and when I'm home I'm either sleeping or with you, and I can't think when I'm with you. Maybe after fire season . . ."

Seeing the anguish on his face, she stopped speaking. His body trembled, and she tried to absorb his pain, knowing that hers would shake her apart if she gave in to it. Physical pain was nothing, compared to the pain of knowing that you were hurting someone else.

Jeff kissed her desperately, feeling as if his world were going up in flames and knowing that he was helpless to stop it.

Suddenly she couldn't keep her hands off him. She wanted to comfort him, but that wasn't enough. She wanted to possess him, to keep him near her always. Desperately she tore at his clothes, unmindful that he was removing hers with as much haste. They fell to the soft bed of moss as Caly pulled him eagerly to her. Jeff entered her quickly, with no preliminaries. She needed none. She was ready for him. Her legs locked him to her, and her nails raked his back in her desperate need.

She gasped breathlessly as he pounded into her, driven by her need and his own. He gripped her hips, raising them higher, and she clung to him, moved with him, urging him on. It was a race. A race to see if the flaming desire would consume them before they reached the summit. A race to see if they would burn up before they exploded.

And explode they did. Together. Into a raging inferno that burned and burned and burned. It didn't consume them; instead it fed them, and they burned again . . . and again . . . until there was nothing left to burn.

They lay trembling in the aftermath of their passion, with no strength or desire to move. Jeff longed to stay inside her forever, and when the time came, he withdrew reluctantly, sadly. The loss tore at his insides, leaving him empty and alone.

He reached out to touch her with a trembling hand, then jerked it away.

"Oh, my Lord. I've hurt you. All I've ever wanted to do was love you, and I've hurt you."

She looked at him in surprise, then glanced down at herself. A few faint bruises covered the tops of her breasts and her upper arms.

"It doesn't matter. I told you before I bruise easily," she said hurriedly, trying to reassure him.

He wasn't listening. His mouth was working, and he turned aside to retch. When he faced her again, he looked like a broken man.

"Please, get dressed," he whispered hoarsely, throwing her shirt to her. "You're so soft, and I . . ."

Picking up his clothes, he stumbled away, no longer the lithe, graceful cowboy. She followed, pulling at his arm.

"Jeff, you have it all wrong."

He broke her grip, but she caught him again and shook him.

"Look at yourself. Your back is covered with scratches, and I bit your shoulder—and look at that." She pointed at a mark on the inside of his thigh. "Now, if you want to call me a bitch or a wildcat, fine. But you are not leaving here feeling guilty because you put a few bruise marks on me."

His eyes began to clear. "You're not a bitch, Caly. You are a beautiful fairy-slipper." His voice was soft.

She smiled at him in relief. "And you are my cowboy. We made wild, passionate love together, Jeff. It's something I'll remember with pleasure for the rest of my life."

His arms went around her, and he rested his forehead against hers. When he finally spoke again, his voice broke.

"And I'll remember it, too, Caly. For all I'll have now are memories." He held her tightly for a moment, then lifted his head slowly. "You'd better get dressed, my . . . Caly. It's time to go home. Do you want to be alone while you lock up?"

Despite his hurt, he was still sensitive to her needs, knowing without being told that she wanted to be alone to say good-bye to her home. How was she ever going to walk away from his love and his caring? she wondered—but she had to.

She drew a deep breath. "Yes, I would."

He nodded. "I'll check out the chopper. Join me when you're ready."

She didn't want to prolong her good-byes, and when she boarded the waiting helicopter a few minutes later, all she took with her were her mother's pictures and her memories.

The trip home seemed endless. Despite her own misery, Caly could feel the pain and suffering in the tight-lipped cowboy beside her. When he pulled his car to a stop in front of the Olsens' yard, Jeff looked absolutely horrible.

Turning to her he said very softly, "I love you, Caly, and I'd give everything I owned to have you by my side for the rest of my life. If I was a braver man, I would accept the fact that you want to be a fire fighter and live with it." He stopped, his mouth working. Swallowing hard he continued. "But I'm not a brave man when it comes to watching the woman I love destroy herself. For that's what you're doing, Caly. This obsession you have for fighting fires will destroy you. Maybe not physically, but it will burn out everything soft that is in you." He wiped a shaking hand over his eyes. "It takes a very brave person to be soft, you know, and it also takes more courage to live than to die." He leaned forward and kissed her tenderly on her lips. "Please, look after yourself. Maybe it doesn't matter to you if you die in a fire. But when you're out there on the lines, please remember that there is someone who loves you and cares what happens to you."

Caly spent the rest of the summer driving herself so hard that she didn't have time to think or to feel. She knew that she was running away from Jeff, and from herself, but she just didn't have any energy to spare. It was all she could do to drag herself from one fire to the next. Every time the siren wailed, she had to reach deeper to find the strength to carry on.

The next time she was home, Myra said quietly, "I saw Jeff in church on Sunday. He asked if you were still alive."

"That's nice."

"He looked awful, thin and haggard."

Caly's face went blank, and the wise woman said no more. Ted arrived later that evening with her possessions in the back of the stock truck. Everything was neatly packed and labeled, and Zeke came out to help move the boxes into his shed until she had a place of her own.

Her photos were in five boxes, and Caly told Ted to leave them on the truck.

"Take them to Jeff and tell them that they're his—and wait a minute, please, I have something else I want to give to him."

Racing upstairs, she found the four rolls of film she had taken during the summer. She'd had no enthusiasm for developing them, so he might as well have them, she thought. Halfway down the stairs she realized that they were mainly of Jeff, and for a moment she regretted her decision. But she didn't dare develop the pictures herself. She might begin to dream.

"Jeff may want these too," she said, handing the film to Ted.

The pictures were the only thing she had that she could give him—except herself, and she couldn't do that.

On the one day Caly had free that summer, she was too keyed up to sit still. In desperation she decided to spend some time exploring Winthrop. Walking up and down the wooden sidewalks of the old western town, she poked around inside the false-fronted stores that now catered to the tourist trade.

At first she was concerned that the local people she'd met when she was with Jeff would ask embarrassing questions about him, but they didn't. They greeted her with friendly smiles, then started talking about the one thing that was foremost in everybody's mind. Rain. The land was scorched and cracked with the drought, and the rivers were almost dry.

Listening to the ranchers talk, Caly couldn't help but worry about Jeff. She knew from what Myra had told her that he was working long hours, hauling water, moving cattle, cutting hay. He must be absolutely exhausted, she realized, and also must be hurting dreadfully as he watched his land dry up and his cattle starve. She wished that she had the courage to be there with him, to share his trouble.

Rising listlessly from the bench in front of Ollie's Restaurant, she wandered down the boardwalk. Bonnie Sue, who was proudly advertising her pregnancy with a bright-blue maternity top and slacks, came out of the Buttery a few feet in front of her.

Surprised, and unwilling to risk a confrontation, Caly turned to walk across the road.

"Wait, Caly. I want to talk to you," Bonnie Sue called, running forward to catch her arm.

Caly swung around and faced her, a tentative smile on her lips. "I wasn't sure you'd speak to me."

"Oh, I've wanted to have a few words with you, all right." Bonnie Sue glared up at Caly, not the least bit intimidated by her height. "In fact, I was going to lambaste you for what you're doing to my brother. But I can see that you're hurting as badly as he is, so I'll hold my tongue. Come on, let's go have a cup of coffee."

She pulled Caly into the Sourdough Baking and Candy Co. and waved her to a table while she ordered from the young woman behind the counter.

Bonnie Sue brought a tray containing three cups of coffee and three cinnamon buns to the table.

"Mother is going to join us," she said quietly.

"What?" Caly half rose from her chair, but Bonnie Sue caught her shoulder and shoved her down.

"She's in the Buttery and sent me out to waylay you. She's afraid you'll refuse to speak to her."

"Me refuse? I thought she didn't like me!"

"You're not one of her favorite people right now, but only because of what you're doing to Jeff." Bonnie Sue put sugar in her coffee as she rattled on. "She admires you, though, and respects you for your independence, and I think she'd come to love you if you'd let her. I know—"

She broke off as Patricia entered the shop, nodded to the woman behind the counter, and slid into the empty chair at the table.

There wasn't a hair out of place in her smooth coiffure, and she looked as dainty and beautiful as ever, making Caly feel like a clodhopper.

Patricia studied Caly carefully as she spoke. "Hello, Caly. I'm sorry I tricked you into meeting me, but I had to talk to you."

Caly nodded and, trying to be nonchalant, forced herself to take a bite of the huge cinnamon bun. It tasted like ashes.

Patricia also seemed to find her bun lacking, and her hands were trembling as she set down her fork and picked up her coffee cup. Suddenly Caly realized that Patricia was just as nervous as she was, and she gathered up enough courage to smile shyly at the older woman.

When Patricia spoke again, her words flowed like a tinkling waterfall.

"I love Jeff, and it hurts me to see him so unhappy. I know that he loves you and wants to marry you, and I want to know if you have refused to marry him because of me." She touched the paper napkin to her lips. "Because if that's the case, I'll leave the ranch. It is important to me, but not as important as Jeff's happiness."

Caly sat there feeling overwhelmed. "But that isn't the reason I've refused to marry him, Mrs. Adams," she said hurriedly. "And if I did marry Jeff, I would never want or expect you to leave your home."

"I think you should know that I'll be leaving regardless of what you decide to do. I . . ." A delicate shade of pink colored Patricia's cheeks. "I'm getting married again."

"To Bill?" Caly guessed, remembering the way he had looked at her the day of the rodeo.

"Yes. And we plan to go traveling for a few years."

"That's wonderful. I'm so pleased for you and for Bill. I hope you'll both be very happy."

"We are, and that's why I want, more than anything else in the world, for Jeff to be happy too. Why won't you marry him, Caly? What's so important that it keeps you away from the man who loves you . . . who would give his life for you?" Patricia's eyes glittered with unshed tears, and Bonnie Sue was dabbing at hers.

Caly gulped. "I . . . Jeff wants me to give up fighting fires. I can't do that yet."

"But why? Are you the type of woman who feels she has to put her career before her husband?"

"No. It's not that." She paused, wanting to explain

but not knowing how. "I—My parents died in a fire . . . and I made a promise . . . and I have to keep fighting them. It's my way of honoring their memory."

Patricia reached across the table and took Caly's hand in her strong grip.

"I understand, my dear, but I don't believe your mother would want you to honor her that way." She squeezed Caly's hand, looking at Bonnie Sue and back to her. "I know I wouldn't, if I were she. I'd want you to be happy."

"I'm sorry, Mrs. Adams. I just can't talk about it anymore." Freeing her hand, she rose to her feet. "I . . . I . . . I'm sorry. I have to go now."

Ignoring Patricia's call, she rushed out the door, concerned only about escaping from everyone who knew that Jeff loved her.

That evening she and three other Smokejumpers were sent to Alaska to pack cargo chutes on a big fire, and it was the first of September before she set foot on the North Cascades Smokejumpers base again.

Because of mechanical problems with the plane, it was dawn before they arrived home, and Caly had only enough energy left to crawl into an empty bed in one of the bunkhouses before collapsing into an exhausted sleep.

She woke up late in the afternoon to find a corsage of tiny pink orchids on the night table. Leaning over, she picked up the corsage, cradling it in her hand as tears blurred her vision.

Finally she noticed a small envelope on the nightstand. Ripping it open, she blinked back the tears and read the message on the enclosed card.

My beloved Calypso,
    The wild Calypso orchids are no longer in bloom, so I'm sending you this orchid instead. Although it

isn't the real thing, it still reminds me of you. So vibrant and beautiful. So sweet and soft. I hope it will also remind you of the beauty around you and of the beauty we have shared.

Take care of yourself and remember there is someone who loves you.

Jeff

Slowly, large tears rolled down Caly's cheeks, dropping unnoticed on the flowers as she cried for the first time since she was seven. Like a heavy downpour, the tears washed through her entire body and into every hidden corner of her mind, taking with them all her hurt and anger and fears.

When the storm passed she felt soft inside, like the flowers she was still holding.

She knew that she was finally brave enough to face herself. Jeff had been right. She had never been afraid of dying, only of living. Underneath, all along, she had expected to die fighting a forest fire. That was why she had no plans for the future, no dreams.

Now she had Jeff, the cowboy who loved her so much that he continued to give to her despite his pain, the cowboy who'd known that her relentless vendetta against the raging fires was destroying her inch by inch and had cared enough to do something about it. He had given her beauty and softness—and dreams.

So what was she going to do about it?

Was she going to keep this prince among men, her Virginian, out of her life forever? Or was she brave enough to admit that she loved him? Brave enough to admit that she hated fighting fires and that she wanted to do something different with her life?

She wanted to create beauty, not fight with all her heart and soul while another beautiful forest was ravaged by fire.

Could she do it? Could she create beauty? Could she find out who she really was?

Yes. She could do it. She could do anything she put her mind to. She knew what her physical capabilities were. Time and time again, she had stretched them to their limits and beyond.

Now was the time to explore the heights and depths and the horizons of her love, and Jeff would help her.

Jeff hadn't asked her to be brave or strong. All he had asked was that she be soft enough to love, soft enough to cry, soft enough to grow. And she knew that Jeff would give her the freedom to grow.

She lay there, holding the corsage and staring at the orchids. Yes, she loved Jeff. She would love him until the day she died. Somehow she knew that her mother would be pleased with her decision. Because her mother, too, had chosen love.

She smiled happily, confidently. She would go to Jeff and tell him that she loved him.

Then a feeling of dismay swept over her as she remembered that she'd never told Jeff that she loved him. He'd told her so many times, but she had never spoken those words.

Less than an hour later Caly realized, with dawning horror, that she might have waited too long to tell Jeff that she loved him.

Ten

For the first time since waking, Caly became aware that there was activity outside the barracks. A helicopter thumped overhead, and she realized that choppers had been coming and going steadily. At least three trucks roared by on the road, and the slamming of doors and the sound of voices indicated that people were arriving at the base. There must have been a fire somewhere. She knew she should get up and see what was happening.

But she didn't want to go out on another fire, she thought in rebellion. She wanted to find Jeff and tell him that she loved him.

Climbing out of bed, she pulled on her Nomex pants and shirt and headed for the bathroom. Moments later, she dragged herself across the tarmac to the office. Fire crews stood around in groups, obviously waiting for transport. Caly didn't recognize any of the faces and decided that the other Smokejumpers must already have been out on a fire.

Nodding at the men who were hanging around outside the office, she made her way into the radio room.

Zeke was standing at the staging map, discussing

the fires with a burly crew boss. He acknowledged her presence with a wave at the empty chair behind the desk.

Caly sat on the edge of the chair, waiting. Her anxiety soared as Zeke ushered the man out the door and closed it before turning toward her.

"Glad you're here, Red. I was 'bout to send someone over to rouse you."

"What's happening? Where is everyone?"

"Out on fires. Most of northern Washington is burning. We have fires here, here, and here." His stubby finger stabbed angrily at the map. "There's a big one at Carleton. We've had to evacuate the Bensen Creek and Texas Creek areas, and close the highway between Twisp and Carleton. But that's not the reason I wanted you."

Zeke rubbed his hand across the back of his bald head, a sure sign that he was worried.

"I may need you to make a medical jump. We've got two hikers overdue. Jeff is out in his chopper, looking for them."

"Jeff?" Caly gripped the edge of the desk, trying to ignore the nerve-tingling feeling that something awful was going to happen.

"Yeah. He's part of the search-and-rescue unit of the Okanogan sheriff's posse, you know?"

"No. I didn't know." It didn't surprise her, though.

"Sure hope he finds them and gets them out by nightfall." Zeke rubbed his bald spot again. "There's no telling where they are in relation to the fire."

"What fire?" The room swung crazily, and Caly was thankful that she was sitting down. Fear sloshed into the pit of her stomach like a gallon of sour milk.

"This one." Zeke jabbed the map. "Chances are, they're nowhere near it." He turned around to study her. "But someone might be hurt, and if Jeff can't get in to pick them up, you may have to make a rescue jump."

"I'll get my gear ready," she mumbled, rising slowly

to her feet. She staggered slightly on the way to the door, and Zeke eyed her sharply.

"Anything wrong?"

"No. Nothing."

But everything was wrong. The bottom was dropping out of her world. Jeff was out there, flying low in smoke-shrouded mountains, looking for lost hikers. And if he found them, he was going to try to land in that godawful terrain and pick them up. No, nothing was wrong. Jeff just might die, that was all. Tears blurred her eyes, and she brushed them away angrily.

In a daze she packed her equipment, replacing her ditty bag with the first-aid kit and checking that all was in order with her harness and suit. Then, forcing herself to think of all possibilities, she went over to the fire cache and, hauling out a six-man fire pack and chute, piled them in a wheelbarrow.

She entered the radio room just as Zeke was clearing the channels.

"That was Jeff. He's spotted them and is going in after them." He rubbed the back of his head again and moved over to the map.

"What's the problem?" Caly asked, bracing herself for the bad news.

"They're in Windy Gap. Here." His finger stabbed the spot. "It's actually a shoulder between two mountains. It's a bitch of a place, with sheer cliffs on both sides."

Caly's mouth was as dry as dust. "And?"

"Both mountains are on fire."

Caly sank into a nearby chair as her knees buckled. It was over ninety degrees in the room, but her sweat was ice-cold. She shivered.

"He'll get them out," Zeke muttered. "We'll hear from him in a few minutes, you'll see."

The second hand on the large clock jogged around slowly—fifteen times. As each minute crept by, Caly was more and more certain that Jeff was dead. It was four-thirty on a blistering afternoon, and Jeff was dead.

At last she turned wide, frightened eyes to Zeke, who had been busy making notes, talking to people on the phone, and keeping his airwaves free so Jeff could radio in.

"We should've heard from him by now."

Zeke glanced up. "Yeah," he agreed slowly.

"He must have crashed." Pushing herself to her feet, she leaned on the desk, pleading with Zeke. "I can't sit here any longer. I have to go after him. I love him. I just can't sit here and let him die."

There, she'd said it. She had finally told someone she loved Jeff. But why couldn't that someone have been her beloved cowboy?

"Yeah, well, I'll fly you out to the Gap in a few minutes." He leveled a stern look at her. "But I won't let you jump till we take a look-see at the site. I can't let you risk your life if there's no hope."

No hope. No hope. The words rang through Caly's mind like a death knell. She clasped her hands tightly together, trying to stop them from trembling.

"Hell, Red. I didn't mean for it to sound that way." Vaguely Caly realized that Zeke was offering her sympathy. "But dammit all, I think you should be prepared for the worst." His voice became crisp again as he started issuing orders. "Pete'll be here in five minutes to take over, and I want you ready to go. We'll take the spotter plane. Now, move it."

With a supreme effort, Caly forced her mind and body to start functioning again. In the fire cache she stuffed pitons, snap links, and extra ropes into four climber's packs, strapped them to the fire pack, and pushed the wheelbarrow out to the high-winged Cessna 172, which was sitting on the tarmac. Mel, the regular pilot, had taken off the door and was removing the passenger seat, turning it into a jump plane. As he began loading her cargo, she ran over to the loft and the quick-suit-up rack.

Never had it taken her so long to suit up, but she must have dressed faster than she thought, because she was back at the plane before Zeke arrived. She was grateful that Zeke was turning over the fire operations to Pete, his second in command, and would be flying her. He was an ace pilot, and often threatened to give up managing the base and go back to flying.

"Still no word?" she asked as he checked over her gear.

"Nope. Pete will radio us if he hears anything."

By the time Caly had strapped herself into the seat behind Zeke, he was taxiing for takeoff. Once airborne, Caly realized that it was going to be one dickens of a ride. The small plane bucked through the turbulent late-afternoon sky. Caly barely noticed the bone-jarring, flesh-bruising jolts and bangs. Her concentration was fixed totally on Jeff.

Thank goodness she had taken the medical-technician course, she thought again. At least she wouldn't feel so helpless if Jeff were hurt. But what if he were dead? She shuddered, remembering the two previous crash sites she'd jumped. There had been no survivors.

She couldn't think about that. Jeff had to be alive. Please, God, let him be alive. Let her have the chance to tell him she loved him. That was all she asked.

Zeke weaved the plane through the smoke-shrouded Cascades to the gap in the mountain, where her love was waiting for death.

Thick black smoke boiled over the mountain. Below it, orange flames licked hungrily at the treetops. The wind had pushed the fire down the mountain to within a quarter mile of the gap, but it already had hurled a flaming torch into the forest on the lower bench, cutting off retreat in that direction. Sheer granite cliffs dropped away from either side of the gap.

There was no escape.

Zeke made a slow turn and brought the plane in

from the north, flying low over the small meadow that crossed the center of the gap. Jeff's helicopter lay on its side, the rotor dug into the ground.

Two people were standing a short distance from it, waving up at the plane. The third figure was lying on the ground, and Caly had time to see that it was Jeff, before the plane passed over the gap.

The nightmare was reality. Jeff was hurt. He might be dead. She had to go to him.

Zeke circled higher. "I'll call in the air tankers. They can make a couple of drops before dark," he shouted over his shoulder.

Caly watched the ground in misery as Zeke radioed the base.

"Damn. They aren't available. Omak just ran out of fuel. They have to go back to Wenachee. I've put in a priority call, but it'll take them a couple of hours to refuel, reload, and get here," Zeke yelled over the noise of the wind blowing through the open door.

Caly wasn't surprised at the news. The Omak airport was set up only as an emergency base, and from all reports, it had been used heavily that day.

She couldn't wait until the air tankers arrived.

"They don't have two hours. I have to jump. Now," she yelled back.

"We'll see. Drop the streamers on the next pass."

She did. Zeke shook his head as he watched them swirl to the ground. The wind was roaring through the gap at gale force.

"You can't jump in that."

"I have to. I'm the only hope they've got."

"We'll drop the fire pack first."

Caly unbuckled her seat belt and crawled over the box so she could push it out the door.

Because of the high wind and the small clearing, they were going to drop it as low as possible, but they'd have to be right on the money. Tensely Caly waited for

Zeke's signal. When it came, she shoved the box out, pulled the rip cord, and prayed.

They circled, watching the pack land in the trees near the clearing and crash its way through the underbrush to the ground.

"I'm next," Caly yelled, crouching in the open door.

"Shouldn't let you go, but you're right. They need you down there. Good luck, Red."

Caly smiled at him, then concentrated on the jump. Normally the parachute was attached to a static line that automatically pulled the cord as she left the plane. But this time she had to pull her own cord. Because of the wind, she was jumping from a lower altitude, relying on a quick descent to keep her from being blown off the mountain.

At Zeke's shouted "Go," she shoved off.

"One thousand . . . two thousand . . . three thousand . . . four thousand," she counted quickly.

She pulled the cord, heard the whoosh, and braced for the jolt.

She looked up and saw the red-and-white canopy above her.

She felt the hot air pulling at her, buffeting her, lifting her—away from the meadow, toward the cliff.

She tucked and rolled on landing, then pulled the release harness and watched as the chute billowed over the edge of the mountain.

Scrambling to her feet, she sprinted to the man she loved.

The two hikers, middle-aged men, stood back to give her room as she dropped to her knees at Jeff's side.

"Oh, Jeff, Jeff," she said with a gasp, shucking her glove and touching his face with a trembling hand. Blood matted the hair above his left temple and ran down his colorless cheek. He was so very still. "Don't die on me. Please, don't die." Blindly she pulled off her helmet and lay her head against Jeff's. She needed to be close to him, to hold him, to touch him. Even if he was dead.

"I'm a doctor," the tall, white-haired man said quietly as he knelt beside her. "He's still alive, but he's got a concussion and a broken left arm."

A wave of relief swept through Caly, leaving her shaken. He was still alive. Thank you, dear God. Thank you, she said silently.

She had to check for herself that Jeff was alive, and she quickly swept her hands and gaze over his body. His left arm lay at an odd angle on his chest, which rose and fell steadily. Yes, he was alive, she realized.

"Miss." The doctor's voice brought her back to reality, and she lifted her gaze to him.

"He'll be okay. I promise." He smiled at her reassuringly. "But if that's a first-aid kit you're carrying, I'll bandage his head and immobilize his arm."

Pulling herself together, she unhooked the bag and handed it over to the doctor, but she couldn't make herself relinquish her place at Jeff's side. All she wanted to do was to hold him. She gently lifted Jeff's head and held it while the doctor swiftly wound a bandage around it. Unconsciously she whistled an out-of-tune version of "Moon River" as visions of Jeff floated through her mind. Jeff walking through the forest, his body strong and lithe. Jeff lying above her, laughing and loving.

His eyelids fluttered, and he moved his head against her hand. She thought she heard him whisper "Calypso" but couldn't be sure.

As they worked on Jeff's arm, she vaguely was aware that the men were trying to explain what had happened.

"A damn downdraft hit him when he was landing. Didn't have a chance," a bald man with a florid complexion and a big, red-veined nose said.

"We pulled him out and brought him over here in case it blew up," the doctor continued.

"Are they going to send in another helicopter?"

Caly spared the nose a glance. "No. But a water bomber is coming in a couple of hours."

"Holy cow. A couple of hours." He wrung his hands. "We'll be dead by then."

He was right. Jeff was alive now, but they'd be burned to death if she didn't get her act together. Reaching down deep inside herself, she found the courage to go on. Did love make you stronger? Did love give you the extra strength you needed in times of crisis? Somehow she knew that it did.

Rising to her feet, she focused her attention on the noise, heat, smoke, and flames of the approaching fire. It was descending on them much faster than even Zeke had expected. They didn't have much time.

Twenty minutes later they were hanging over the side of the mountain, with two pitons and two sets of ropes holding each person. In addition they were belayed together, and the ropes above had been soaked with the water from the fire pack.

They had dressed Jeff in her jump suit and harness, and he was hanging against the mountain with his head cradled on her shoulder. She straddled him, her feet wedged into a crack and her hands gripping the rocks to keep his body from swinging in the wind.

He was still unconscious, but he was alive, and he was in her arms—and that was all that mattered just then.

She barely was aware of the roar of the fire above and the resounding cannon shots as the giant trees fell like matchsticks. Acrid smoke swirled down around them, choking them. Boulders tumbled over the cliff, bouncing above, then below them. Flaming torches lanced by, but mercifully they were protected by the slant of the slope above them.

Intense heat enveloped them, scorching their skin and singeing their hair as the fireball flashed through Windy Gap.

The heart of the fire thundered past, and with its passing came hope. They were going to live.

Slowly they began to move, coughing, choking, joking, even laughing in relief.

Jeff stirred, his head rolling back against the padded collar of the jump suit.

"Don't move, Jeff," Caly said, her hands cradling his head. "You're hanging on the side of a mountain."

"Caly?" he whispered, opening his eyes. They were clouded for a moment, then cleared as he recognized her. Slowly he raised his good arm to her waist.

"Be still, my love. I'll keep you safe."

"You're here? Why did you come?" he asked hoarsely.

"Because I love you." There, she had finally said it.

"You love me?" The doubt and confusion in his voice made Caly want to cry, but she looked bravely into his eyes, deliberately letting him see the depths of her soul.

"Yes. I love you," she said, choking back her tears.

"Caly . . ." His lips trembled in a weak smile, and his eyes shone with happiness as he saw, and believed. "You . . . you . . . didn't have to jump . . . into the middle of a fire . . . to tell me."

"I couldn't wait." She gave a high, short little laugh. "And you know me. I always jump into things without thinking."

"My . . . my . . . Calypso . . . I . . ." He closed his eyes.

"But this time, my love, I didn't jump without thinking," she continued in a rush, afraid that he would pass out again before she'd told him everything she wanted to say. "I knew exactly what I was doing. I love you and I want to marry you."

His lips moved, but there was no sound, and Caly realized that he had lost consciousness. Although she desperately wanted to know his answer, she knew she would have to wait until he had regained consciousness.

She couldn't wait any longer to kiss him, though. Bracing herself securely against the face of the mountain, she kissed him tenderly, whispering, "I love you" between kisses.

She was still kissing him and whispering, "I love you," when the first air tanker arrived.

She held fast to her love during the rest of the night as she sat with the men in the blackened gap, holding Jeff and praying. With morning light came a helicopter, which airlifted all of them to Seattle.

She held fast to her love as Jeff disappeared into the emergency room, and it sustained her until she was allowed to sit beside his bed.

He looked so white, lying on the white bed with his cast and bandaged head. So white, so still, so defenseless. She wanted to hold him and keep him safe forever and ever.

For the first time she realized just how much agony Jeff had suffered every time she went out on a fire.

What if he had died? How could she have gone on living?

The room was suddenly full as Patricia, Bonnie Sue, Michael, Mary Ellen, Nancy Jane, and Babs arrived. As they held her and kissed her, Caly felt she was part of a family—a loving family, who cared about one another and about her.

As they quietly discussed the details of the fires, Caly realized with a sinking heart that she should go back to help. But what she really wanted to do was to stay with Jeff. Reluctantly she rose to her feet and looked down at him, loving him and wishing that he would regain consciousness so she could at least say good-bye before she left.

Almost as if he could hear her silent plea, he stirred, opened his eyes, and smiled at her.

"Hi, there, Li'l Red." His voice was husky but strong, and his eyes were clear.

Her throat was so tight with tears that she couldn't say anything, and contented herself with carrying his free hand to her lips.

He brushed his fingers against her lips. "Don't look so frightened." He tried a smile. It was weak, but it was a smile. "It'll take more than a 'copter crash to get me out of your life."

"Oh, Jeff," she whispered, and then the rest of the family was crowding around the bed, talking all at once. Jeff smiled at and spoke to all of them, but his gaze kept returning to Caly, and a sense of contentment filled her. He loved his family, but she would come first.

"Are the fires all out?" he finally asked, his eyes caressing her. She shook her head as Bonnie Sue and Mary Ellen babbled on about the severity of the fire situation.

"Then why are you still hanging around here, Li'l Red?" He squeezed her fingers. "You should be out there fighting them."

Caly bent closer, looking for signs of fear and worry in his face. She saw the worry, but she also saw the love and tenderness and trust. Tears blurred her vision, and she blinked them away quickly.

"I had to wait till I could tell you again that I love you," she whispered, kissing him hungrily.

When she finally raised her head, they were both breathless. "I seem to remember hearing you say that a few times on the mountain." His voice was soft and husky.

She smiled at him, her eyes shining. "A few million times, at least."

"And I love you." He brushed his right hand along her cheek. "Take care, now, and when the fires are out, hurry home to me."

•   •   •

During the rest of the week the promise in his voice kept her going as she fought the Barker Mountain fire. By the time it was tamed, it had blackened twenty-five thousand acres, destroyed nineteen homes, and forced the evacuation of five hundred people. Only a last-minute change in the direction of the wind had prevented it from burning the town of Tonasket to the ground.

And by the time it was finally under control, Caly had had enough.

"I quit," she told Zeke as she stumbled off the plane in a state of total exhaustion.

"About time," Zeke said, rubbing the back of his head. "I know you have other plans, Red, but Myra and me will be happy to have you stay with us as long as you want."

Heedless of the other Smokejumpers, she threw her arms around him. "Thanks, Zeke," she said, feeling as if she had just gained a father.

Grinning in pleasure, he led her toward the office. "Come in, Red. Something came for you this morning."

It was a corsage of tiny red orchids.

"He's home?" Caly asked, cradling the orchids in her soot-blackened hand.

"Yep. Got home yesterday," Zeke called after her as she dashed out the door, leaped down the steps, and raced for her motorbike.

Jeff was waiting for her on the porch, sitting in the swing that held such good memories for him. He rose to meet her as she ran up the steps. She looked like a Raggedy Ann doll, with her flaming hair and baggy clothes. She was so thin that he was afraid to hold her too close, in case she broke.

But her arms were strong around him, and there was nothing fragile about the way she kissed him.

Caly stepped back, staring in horror at the orchids, which she'd crushed against his cast.

"Oh, Jeff, I'm sorry. Did I hurt you? The flowers! They were so beautiful."

It was the last straw. Every time she was near him, she did something awful. She raised tear-filled eyes to his.

"Hey, there. No tears. I'm fine, and I don't need the flowers when I have the real thing." Gently he eased her into the swing and sat down beside her. She rested in the cradle of his right arm, feeling as if she finally had come home.

Jeff was content to swing in silence, while she ran her hands over his head and face, making sure that he was all right.

Finally she sighed. "I do love you, you know, Jeff. So very, very much."

"I know you do, Caly, but you didn't have to jump into a forest fire to prove it."

"I wasn't trying to prove anything. All I wanted was to be near you. That's what love is all about, isn't it, Jeff? The need to be with the one you love so much that you'd go to him no matter where he was. Even if he were in the middle of a raging inferno." She shuddered and raised her eyes to his. Suddenly she burrowed against him, sobbing like a heartbroken child. "I almost lost you, Jeff, and I couldn't bear a life without you near."

Jeff held her while she cried, rocking the swing gently as his own tears mingled with hers. Gradually they became aware of the rain plopping on the porch roof.

"Listen," Caly said, raising her head and smiling through her tears. "Even Mother Nature has decided to cry."

Jeff brushed his fingers across her cheeks, wiping away the tears. "I'm glad you feel safe enough to cry in my arms, Caly." He looked at her with his heart in his eyes. "We're making progress."

"I seem to be crying a lot lately." She smiled at him sheepishly. "Maybe you shouldn't send me flowers anymore."

He laughed and pulled her head back onto his chest. "I'll take my chances with the tears."

She lay quietly, listening to the steady beating of his heart. Finally she gathered up enough courage to ask, "Do you remember my asking you to marry me?"

"I remember." His voice was soft and full of love.

"I'm still waiting for an answer."

He hugged her closer. "I want to, Caly . . . so very much. Nothing would make me happier." He paused and the last words were a mere whisper. "But I can't."

"You can't!" she cried in shock and disappointment. She tried to raise her head, but he held her still, speaking quickly before she could say anything more.

"I want you to be very sure of who you are before you marry me, Caly, and I don't think you really know yet, do you?"

She managed to free herself so she could look him straight in the eyes. "I don't need any more time. I know right now, right this very instant, that if I were your wife and the mother of your children, I'd be the happiest woman in the world," she said earnestly.

"That's not enough." His eyes were sad.

"I've decided to give up fire-fighting," she continued in an effort to convince him.

He shook his head, smiling tenderly. "You don't have to give it up, you know. I want you to investigate some other options first. If you decide that you still want to be a fire fighter, then I'll be the husband of a fire fighter."

She looked at him in concern. His head injury must have been worse than she'd thought.

"It won't mean that I'll stop worrying about you, or that I won't die a little every time you go out on a fire," he continued, proving that he still had the ability to read her mind. "But I've been doing a lot of thinking, and I realize that you're like the forest. You need fire as well as water to grow. The main thing is, I want you to be happy, and the only way you'll be happy is if you're happy with yourself, with who you are."

"Oh, Jeff, I still don't know who I am, and I don't know if I'll ever find out," she cried in anguish.

"Will you let me help?"

"Yes," she agreed promptly, proving to them both beyond a shadow of a doubt that she trusted him.

He kissed her lightly, trying to control the jubilation that threatened to overwhelm him. "Thank you, my love." Looking down into her shining eyes, he lost control, claiming her lips in a soul-shattering kiss. They were both shaking when he finally raised his head. "Will you come with me to Seattle on Friday to a show at my sister's gallery?" he asked when he could speak again.

"Friday." She looked at him in puzzlement, wondering what this request had to do with her finding herself. "That's the day after tomorrow. What show do you want me to see?"

"It's called 'Calypso's Journey,' " he said, then held his breath.

It took a moment for his words to sink in. " 'Calypso's Journey'?"

"Yeah."

"A show? You mean my photos are being shown?"

"No. My photos." His breath whooshed out, along with a flood of words. "When you sent them over to me, all I wanted to do was hoard them. But they were too beautiful for me to keep them for myself, and I finally decided that I had to share them. Nancy Jane agreed and is using them as the main theme in her fall show. And I . . ." He faltered to a stop.

"But they aren't good enough to be shown at a major art gallery," Caly objected in bewilderment.

"Nancy Jane thinks they are, and so do I. All I ask is that you come see the show. It might help you decide who you are." His eyes pleaded with her. "Please come, my love."

She looked at him, and saw hope and belief and love. He gave her the courage to whisper, "Yes, I'll come."

"Good." He hugged her close, then released her and kissed her sweetly. "Because I have every intention of marrying you, my Calypso, and I don't want to wait much longer," he murmured against her lips.

Caly basked in the warmth of his love, feeling protected and cherished. But it was two more days before she learned the true meaning of Jeff's brand of love.

Caly knew the dress was responsible for her courage. It was a shimmering creation of blues and greens that Jeff had bought for her because it reminded him of Emerald Lake.

Babs, who was staying at the Alexis Hotel with her, had been shocked when she'd seen it, for although it had long sleeves, the neckline plunged to her waist, and a slit in the front of the ankle-length skirt revealed an indecent length of her shapely legs.

But Caly felt elegant in the dress and knew instinctively that she and Jeff made a striking couple. Jeff was rakishly handsome in a tuxedo, and the black sling, which supported his left arm, gave him aura of danger and mystery.

The dress had given her courage when they went out to dine, but she had tasted very little of the gourmet meal. The dress was now giving her courage as they entered the art gallery near Pioneer Square.

The entire family was there, including Myra and Zeke and Bill, who was holding Patricia with one hand and a cane with the other. Babs dabbed at her eyes before kissing Caly. Bonnie Sue gave her a quick hug, and

Patricia looked at her in awe. Caly realized that they had come to give her support, and a deep feeling of love and gratitude flowed through her.

"Fabulous. Simply fabulous." Babs blew her nose.

"Why didn't you tell me you were so good with a camera, dearie?" Myra asked, her eyes suspiciously wet behind her thick lenses.

Nancy Jane appeared from an inner gallery, beaming. "My dear, everyone is enraptured. Jeff wouldn't let us put price tags on the photos, but already a dozen people have asked for bookings."

"I'll show her around, shall I?" Jeff asked, breaking in on Nancy Jane's explanation.

Tucking her hand under his good arm, he said, "The show is in three parts. The first one's in here." He led her into a room full of her old friends from the cabin at Emerald Lake. She greeted each with delight, thankful that she had given them to her cowboy and overjoyed to see them again. A placard explained each picture, and Caly was astonished that Jeff had remembered so much of what she'd told him during that treasured afternoon in the cabin.

The second gallery portrayed in black and white and vivid color the story of forest fires, and of the men and women who fought them. The collection was dramatic, making a powerful statement about the flaming destruction, the desolate aftermath, and the vibrant rebirth of a forest. It was obvious from the admiration and respect in hushed voices and the unashamed tears in a few eyes that the photos were making a big impact on the patrons. A scrolled sign above the collection dedicated it to the memory of her parents and Big Red.

Caly turned to the silent man at her side, her amber eyes bright with tears. "You're right, Jeff. I can honor my parents in other ways."

Jeff hugged her, giving her time to regain her composure before they moved on.

As they walked toward the third gallery, Caly could feel the tension building in Jeff. She was about to ask him what was wrong, when he turned aside to avoid a man and two women who were coming out of the room, smiling and chatting.

"Wow, I'd sure like to meet the cowboy. What a hunk."

"Do you think she'd take my picture?" the man asked.

"She'd never make you look that sexy, my dear, no matter how good she is—and she's very good." They moved on down the hall, laughing.

Jeff turned back to the door, his shoulders stiff, his face grim. Caly saw panic flicker briefly in his eyes as they entered the room, and then he looked down at her tenderly.

Glancing around the third gallery, Caly gasped in surprise. Entitled "Calypso's Cowboy," the collection revealed the many facets of Jeff: the romantic cowboy, leaning across the saddle horn, smiling at her from his horse; the protector, glaring ferociously down the barrel of a rifle; the victor, riding a white brahman in jubilation; the playmate, standing waist-deep in Emerald Lake, laughing and throwing water in a rainbow around his head; the gentle man, watching the butterfly on his hand with wonder in his eyes; the little boy, looking vulnerable in sleep; the lover, looking sexier than any man had the right to look, lying in bed with hand outstretched and a come-hither smile. There were many more pictures of Jeff: the terrific uncle, indulgent brother, valued friend, and beloved son.

But the one that made Caly's heart turn over was of Jeff the dreamer, watching a sunset, lost in melancholy.

This, then, was love. Jeff's brand of love.

For this very modest, private, intensely proud man loved her so much that he was willing to expose his heart and soul to the rest of the world if it meant she would believe in herself.

And suddenly she did believe in herself. Her photos *were* good.

"You did this for me?" she asked, raising tear-filled eyes to his face. He was flushed with embarrassment, but he was beaming with pride.

"Nancy Jane thought they were your best work," he muttered, chewing on his lip. "She thought that they showed how much you had matured as a photographer, and that the collection wouldn't be complete without them. I—I couldn't stop her from showing them, if they made a difference to the success of your show."

"Oh, Jeff. You're so very . . . very good to me. Thank you," she said.

His love was there for all the world to see, both in the photos and on his face, but he wasn't going to do anything about it. It would be up to her to convince him that he had given her what she was looking for—herself.

Unmindful of the family and patrons, who were waiting breathlessly to see what would happen next, Caly took Jeff's arm and led him from one picture to another, studying them critically.

"They're terrific, aren't they? But only because you're such a handsome model." She turned to him. "But more than that, you're an honorable man, a man who is so sensitive and caring that my heart almost breaks from loving you."

"Caly," he whispered, his hand brushing her cheek gently.

She smiled up at him, her love glowing on her face. "You're the only man I'd ever want to be my husband and the father of our six kids."

"Is this a proposal, my Calypso?" he asked gruffly.

"Yes. But I want to make it clear that I'm not promising to darn your socks or sew on your buttons."

"I don't want you to." He swallowed hard. "I just want to know who's asking me."

She looked deeply into his Emerald-Lake eyes as she answered. "The tomboy who wants to play with your six children, the lover who wants to make them, and the woman who knows who she is and what she wants."

Lacing her fingers behind Jeff's neck, Caly reached up and kissed him.

"I want many things," she whispered against his lips. "But most of all I want to love my cowboy—my Virginian—for the rest of my life."

THE EDITOR'S CORNER

With the very special holiday for romance lovers on the horizon, we're giving you a bouquet of half a dozen long-stemmed LOVESWEPTs next month. And we hope you'll think each of these "roses" is a perfect one of its kind.

We start with the romance of a pure white rose, **IT TAKES A THIEF**, LOVESWEPT #312, by Kay Hooper. As dreamily romantic as the old South in antebellum days, yet with all the panache of a modern-day romantic adventure film, Kay's love story is a delight . . . and yet another in her series that we've informally dubbed "Hagen Strikes Again!" Hero Dane Prescott is as enigmatic as he is handsome. A professional gambler, he would be perfectly at home on a riverboat plying the Mississippi a hundred years ago. But he is very much a man of today. And he has a vital secret . . . one he has shouldered for over a decade. Heroine Jennifer Chantry is a woman with a cause—to regain her family home, Belle Retour, lost by her father in a poker game. When these two meet, even the sultry southern air sizzles. You'll get reacquainted, too, in this story with some of the characters you've met before who revolve around that paunchy devil, Hagen—and you'll learn an intriguing thing or two about him. This fabulous story will also be published in hardcover, so be sure to ask your bookseller to reserve a collector's copy for you.

With the haunting sweetness and excitement of a blush-pink rose, **MS. FORTUNE'S MAN**, LOVESWEPT #313, by Barbara Boswell sweeps you into an emotion-packed universe. Nicole Fortune bounds into world-famous photographer Drake Austin's office and demands money for the support of his child. Drake is a rich and virile heartbreaker who is immediately stopped in his tracks by the breathtaking beauty and warmth of Nicole. The baby isn't his—and soon Nicole knows it—but he's not about to let the girl of his dreams get out of sight. That means he has

(continued)

to get involved with Nicole's eccentric family. Then the fun and the passion really begin. We think you'll find this romance a true charmer.

As dramatic as the symbol of passion, the red-red rose, **WILD HONEY,** LOVESWEPT #314, by Suzanne Forster will leave you breathless. Marc Renaud, a talented, dark, brooding film director, proves utterly irresistible to Sasha McCleod. And she proves equally irresistible to Marc, who knows he shouldn't let himself touch her. But they cannot deny what's between them, and, together, they create a fire storm of passion. Marc harbors a secret anguish; Sasha senses it, and it sears her soul, for she knows it prevents them from fully realizing their love for each other. With this romance of fierce, primitive, yet often tender emotion, we welcome Suzanne as a LOVESWEPT author and look forward to many more of her thrilling stories.

Vivid pink is the color of the rose Tami Hoag gives us in **MISMATCH,** LOVESWEPT #315. When volatile Bronwynn Prescott Pierson leaves her disloyal groom at the altar, she heads straight for Vermont and the dilapidated Victorian house that had meant a loving home to her in her childhood. The neighbor who finds her in distress just happens to be the most devastatingly handsome hunk of the decade, Wade Grayson. He's determined to protect her; she's determined to free him from his preoccupation with working night and day. Together they are enchanting . . . then her "ex" shows up, followed by a pack of news hounds, and all heck breaks loose. As always, Tami gives us a whimsical, memorable romance full of humor and stormy passion.

Sparkling like a dew-covered yellow rose, **DIAMOND IN THE ROUGH,** LOVESWEPT #316, is full of the romantic comedy typical of Doris Parmett's stories. When Detective Dan Murdoch pushes his way into Millie Gordon's car and claims she's crashed his stakeout, she knows she's in trouble with the law . . . or, rather, the

(continued)

lawman! Dan's just too virile, too attractive for his own good. When she's finally ready to admit that it's love she feels, Dan gets last-minute cold feet. Yet Millie insists he's a true hero and writes a book about him to prove it. In a surprising and thrilling climax, the lady gets her man . . . and you won't soon forget how she does it.

As delicate and exquisite as the quaint Talisman rose is Joan Elliott Pickart's contribution to your Valentine's Day reading pleasure. **RIDDLES AND RHYMES**, LOVE-SWEPT #317, gives us the return of wonderful Finn O'Casey and gives him a love story fit for his daring family. Finn discovers Liberty Shaw in the stacks of his favorite old bookstore . . . and he loses his heart in an instant. She is his potent fantasy come to life, and he can't believe his luck in finding her in one of his special haunts. But he is shocked to learn that the outrageous and loveable older woman who owned the bookstore has died, that Liberty is her niece, and that there is a mystery that puts his new lady in danger. In midsummer nights of sheer ecstasy Liberty and Finn find love . . . and danger. A rich and funny and exciting love story from Joan.

Have a wonderful holiday with your LOVESWEPT bouquet.

And do remember to drop us a line. We always enjoy hearing from you.

With every good wish,

Carolyn Nichols

Carolyn Nichols
Editor
LOVESWEPT
Bantam Books
666 Fifth Avenue
New York, NY 10103

Special Offer
Buy a Bantam Book
for only 50¢.

Now you can have Bantam's catalog filled with hundreds of titles plus take advantage of our unique and exciting bonus book offer. A special offer which gives you the opportunity to purchase a Bantam book for only 50¢. Here's how!

By ordering any five books at the regular price per order, you can also choose any other single book listed (up to a $5.95 value) for just 50¢. Some restrictions do apply, but for further details why not send for Bantam's catalog of titles today!

Just send us your name and address and we will send you a catalog!

BANTAM BOOKS, INC.
P.O. Box 1006, South Holland, Ill. 60473

Mr./Mrs./Ms. _____
(please print)

Address _____

City _____ State _____ Zip _____

FC(A)—10/87

Please allow four to six weeks for delivery.

THE DELANEY DYNASTY

Men and women whose loves and passions are so glorious it takes many great romance novels by three bestselling authors to tell their tempestuous stories.

THE SHAMROCK TRINITY